She went back in time to rescue him. She never counted on falling in love...

Alma Whitecrow prefers hunting and fishing with men, not romancing them. But hearing about the roguishly handsome *coureur de bois*, who saved her sister from the Dakota, haunts her thoughts and dreams. Well-versed in surviving the wilds, Alma resolves to travel to the mid-eighteenth century, as her sister once did, to save the man from impending death.

Charlot Baudelaire thumbs his nose at society's expectations, content living as a loner, trading with people he calls the *Saulters*. If he needs a woman for the night, there is always a willing maiden. What he doesn't expect is a spunky and stubborn female warrior to challenge him.

Charlot is not the man Alma dreamed about, and Alma is not the kind of woman Charlot pursues. But the longer they are together, the more drawn to each other they become, until Alma faces the biggest decision of her life. Stay with a man who may never reciprocate her love, or return to her Ojibway home and bland existence.

BORN LIKE THIS
Copyright © 2025 MAGGIE BLACKBIRD
ISBN: 978-1-4874-4372-6
Cover art by MARTINE JARDIN

Published by eXtasy Books Inc

Look for us online at:
www.eXtasybooks.com

BORN LIKE THIS
MAIZMERIZED - 2

By

MAGGIE BLACKBIRD

Dedication

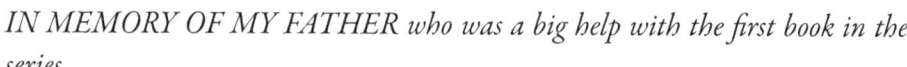

IN MEMORY OF MY FATHER who was a big help with the first book in the series.

Thank you to my husband and the Mals for your love and support. Also, thank you to Extasy Books for always believing in my work.

Chapter One: Twisted Little Sister

"I CAN'T BELIEVE YOU left him there to die." Alma's stomach shouldn't sour at the thought, but her belly did anyway. She'd been unable to stop thinking about the fate of Charlot Baudelaire after hearing the story last year.

"There was nothing I could do." Edie gasped, her dark eyes widening. "I told you a million times the Dakota were attacking us. I was lucky I got out of there." She tossed a chocolate bar and a bag of chips into one of the many Halloween bags she'd hand out to the trick-or-treaters in the evening. "I'm not going to talk to you about this anymore. We talked about it enough this past year."

The amount of defensiveness in her older sister's voice forced Alma to fold her arms. Sure, Edie had gotten out safely, but there had to be a way to save the man who'd put his life on the line for her sister.

Guilt expanded inside Alma's chest.

Maybe she shouldn't have badgered Edie about Charlot again, the handsome man who'd risked his life to save her sister. A man her brother-in-law had described as sly with an eye for the pretty girls, and highly independent since he'd operated as a *coureur de bois*, thumbing his nose at the system New France had established for formal trade with Alma's people, but it came with rules, payment, and a proper license. Edie had said Charlot spat on such a system, declaring nobody could tell him who he could trade with and when.

Green eyes, sandy brown hair, and a handsome face was how Edie had described Charlot to Alma.

There was no way and no how she could purge him from her mind, even though a year had passed since her sister had gone into a corn maze on Halloween night, which had transported Edie back to the mid-eighteenth century. Nobody on the rez knew what had happened, only their family, since their grandfather had insisted they keep quiet because their Ojibway community wouldn't believe them.

Learning about the corn maze not only haunted Alma while awake, but also when she slept, but the mystical place had vanished after Edie returned to the present time thanks to Charlot, who'd bravely stood his ground against the Dakota while pushing Edie through dancing flames that returned her to the maze. Once Edie had found her way out, the mysterious place had simply disappeared.

Alma hadn't planned on attending anything or dressing up this Halloween night. Sure, parties were happening, and one of her brothers had driven in from Winnipeg to celebrate the haunting evening, but she'd passed. Probably because the plan she'd conjured kept cropping up in her mind.

Plus, it'd be a lame party she'd attend. Everything in her world was lame these days. Even the current situation she found herself in—attending the *Anishinaabe* Education Institution located on one of the reserves in their Treaty area, going for her Bachelor of Arts. But her heart wasn't in her studies. She'd only enrolled because she had to do something. With Edie finishing her degree online since she had a new baby to care for, Alma couldn't sit around doing nothing.

She toyed with her nephew's rattle. The infant sat in his baby chair at the kitchen table, cooing at his mother bagging candy.

Alma had already packed the provisions she'd need if she found the corn maze and ventured into the past. Maybe the mysterious skeletal creature Edie had spoken about might reappear and offer Alma the chance to save Charlot? They couldn't just let him die.

She was an excellent hunter and had the best of all hunting dogs. Grandpa had taught her everything about the outdoors while helping her train Theodore. Perhaps that was why she found girls her age boring. Even in high school, they'd looked at her as *the misfit* because she was more interested in hunting and fishing or learning medicine when Great-Grandpa took her into the bush to help him pick plants so he could make his favorite batch of Tamarac tea.

She stood.

"Where're you going?" Edie helplessly gaped at the mounds of candy needing to be bagged. "You promised to help me get ready for the kids."

"I have to study for a test," Alma lied. She stole a mini chocolate bar from the bunch on the table. "It won't take you long."

Edie sighed. "You have to stay in the present. Thinking about Charlot—"

"I'm not thinking about him." A fistful of annoyance heated Alma's face.

"You just finished saying you can't believe he died. Of course you're thinking about him."

Alma edged to the door where she'd left her jacket and shoes. "I told you I need to study for a test. I gotta go. I'll stop by tomorrow."

"Go ahead. I'll finish this by myself." Edie furrowed her brows.

"Adrian will be home soon," Alma said to pacify her sister. "He's your husband. He'll help you."

"My husband has more important things to do than bag candy. He works full-time and is also a part-time student."

A smidgen of guilt reared its ugly head, but Alma mentally stomped all over her conscience. "I gotta go. Bye." She dashed to the mudroom, where she slipped on her shoes and jacket. Before her sister could grumble another word, Alma bolted out the back door straight into the setting sun.

She jumped off the steps and raced to Mom's car. Time was on her side. No trick-or-treaters were about yet. She drove off, making the turn at Moose Drive. No one in her family understood her urgency to save someone she'd never met, but Alma couldn't help herself. A man's life was on the line.

Ever since Edie had returned, pregnant with her tale about going back in time where she'd met Adrian, who'd lived as a warrior named Thunder Bear and had referred to Edie as Fire Woman, unearthing the maze had become Alma's obsession.

Although Edie insisted everything had worked out perfectly since her true love was reincarnated as Adrian, there remained unfinished business in the past. Alma's brain kept calling her crazy because no matter how many times she'd driven to the wide-open field located before the town of Morson, no corn maze had surfaced.

Halloween. Maybe the maze only appeared during a full moon on this special night? Edie had been on her way to a Halloween party when she'd encountered the maze. Maybe Alma would finally find the mystical place.

Alma didn't have to worry about missing the Grandmother Moon ceremony either, because they were holding the event tomorrow evening, since the women who attended were busy taking their children out for candy or handing out treats to the goblins and ghosts.

The disguise Alma had devised might also go unnoticed, thanks to the costumed people running about. She must try. Someone had to save Charlot Baudelaire.

"WHAT'RE YOU DOING?" Mom asked in her ever-suspicious tone.

After Edie had gone missing, Mom was forever checking on them, even though Big Sis was fine. Since their two older brothers lived in Winnipeg, they had luckily escaped Mom's eagle eye. But with Devon home for the Halloween celebrations, he was probably getting the lecture now.

"I'm getting dressed for a party." If Alma kept up with the lies, her nose would grow longer than Pinocchio's. She made sure to lock the door to her bedroom.

Many times, Grandpa had teasingly referred to her as *Ogichidaa-kwe*, which he said translated to *strong-spirited woman* in *Anishinaabemowin*. But the English language translated the word to *female warrior*.

Maybe she was like Chief Earth Woman, meant to defy convention

In the days of her ancestors, Earth Woman had chosen to take up arms alongside her fellow warriors against the Dakota when the Ojibway had engaged in battle with them over this land. Earth Woman had supplied the men with many dream visions on how to defeat the Dakota.

The very war Alma wanted to return to and save Charlot.

She unlocked the cabinet where she stored the rifle Grandpa had gifted her with on her eighteenth birthday. Her ammo was also stored there. She removed both. The backpack rested on the floor, stuffed with what she'd need in case she managed to travel through the maze to find Charlot.

Theodore's big frame took up the twin bed. His tongue hung out, his soulful eyes full of curiosity. "You can't come with me." She kept rifling through the cabinet. "It's too dangerous. I don't want to chance you getting hurt, no matter how awesome you are as a hunting companion."

She straightened and checked her reflection in the dresser's mirror. A fur cap to cover her ears and keep them warm. Her favorite camouflage jacket, which she used for hunting. She wouldn't wear her bright orange safety vest this time, though. Matching pants. Sturdy boots. Layers beneath the jacket. Her ammo clip to hold her bullets, a canteen of fresh water, and survival gear were strapped to her belt. She was set to go.

At least when she traveled back in time, people would treat her as a true eighteen-year-old, instead of an oversized baby as they did in the twenty-first century. What was it with adults anyway? Why did they fear letting their kids grow up? It was so annoying.

During the Great War, eighteen-year-olds had been treated as adults. Heck, her great-grandmother, whom she'd been named after, had married at seventeen and had her first child at eighteen in the late nineteen forties.

Alma grabbed her rifle and backpack.

A knock came at the front door.

Perfect. With Mom busy handing out treats, she wouldn't notice Alma slipping away.

She edged out of her bedroom and tiptoed across the living room to get to the utility room. Mom had the door open, busily greeting kids holding out their pillowcases for candy. A motley group of ghosts, zombies, witches, and dragons.

The breaths coming from Theodore were heavy on Alma's backside, and she stiffened.

She'd shoo him away after. Right then, she had to sneak her way outside.

The TV blared from her parents' bedroom near the back entrance, but Dad was probably too wrapped up in the news to notice her.

Alma lifted Mom's key fob off the rack where everyone kept their stash. This was working out better than she had planned.

To fit everything through the entranceway, Alma had to open the back door wide, which gave Theodore the opportunity to bound past her. Keeping her annoyed scream to herself, she shut the door, glaring at the dog.

"You can't come. Stay." She used her firmest voice.

Theodore trotted to the car.

Alams stomped after him. "Steps. Go back." She hadn't known him to disobey before. He darn well knew disobedience meant pain or death when they were out hunting.

He waited at the passenger door.

"You're not coming." She stashed her supplies and her rifle in the trunk. "Go back."

Theodore did nothing.

"Welp, you can stand here all night, but I'm leaving." Alma opened the driver's side door.

Theodore had snuck around the car. Before she could scamper inside, he bounded past her, his big rump taking up any chance she had of sneaking in first.

He wiggled his way to the passenger seat, almost unable to fit since he was one hundred and fifty pounds.

If this wasn't fate telling her to quit being an idiot and get the hell inside, she didn't know what was. Because if she fought to get Theodore out of the car, she'd raise the alarm, and Mom would bust her.

Yet, how could she take her dog into an unknown, dangerous situation? Even worse, she had no provisions for him. Well, his harness was forever stowed in her hunting pack, so at least he had that. But she didn't have food for him.

"Dammit." She banged the steering wheel.

"Alma?" Mom's shout reached the outdoors.

Shit, she had to get out of here. With a quick turn of the key, she backed the car from the driveway and sped away.

She glared at her dog. "You're bad. Very bad."

Theodore cocked his head.

"Never mind." She had to focus on the trip, albeit with an unexpected partner thanks to her stubborn dog.

It'd take about forty-five minutes to reach the area Edie had shown her. She'd have to turn off the highway and head up the road leading to Morson, the little village a stone's throw from the biggest lake in the area—Lake of the Woods.

The moon cast a silver glow against the night sky, giving it a shade of midnight blue.

More trick-or-treaters peppered the roads.

She waved at the kids before turning off the main road of the reserve and onto the highway. Excitement bubbled in her chest. It had to happen tonight. For sure, the corn maze would appear.

After driving for a good half hour with Theodore operating as lookout, she reached the turn-off to Morson. She took the car over the railroad tracks and started down the oiled road. The closer she got, the faster her heart raced.

When she reached the turn where the field was supposed to be, what the moon shone down on pretty much slapped her across the face.

Surreal.

It did exist.

Truly existed.

Before her was the corn maze just as Edie had described. A big, beautiful, but creepy-looking place with light in the front coming from torches...maybe.

Alma steered the car across the trampled grass leading to the maze. Lit pumpkins sat on bales of hay and straw. Two torches illuminated the entrance. But she didn't spy the skeleton-like creature Edie had mentioned, believing it to be *Mandaamin*, the corn spirit of the Ojibway.

She switched off the car. Just as she opened the door, Theodore banged up against her, pushing her from the vehicle. "Will you give me a second?" She snorted.

As she rounded the car, he dogged her heels.

She popped the trunk to retrieve the supplies.

Please let the creature be here.

Please.

She snatched her rifle and backpack with her sleeping bag tied to the bottom.

Gun in hand, she approached the entrance.

Like a good boy, Theodore stayed behind, waiting for her command.

The closer she got, the faster her breathing became.

Then he appeared—a skeleton dressed in a checkered shirt, worn jeans, and a straw hat.

Alma stumbled backward, almost banging into Theodore.

The creature lifted his head, but not enough to get a peek at his face.

Alive?

How strange that something which appeared dead could live.

He looked as withered as dry corn husks.

She swallowed, telling herself there was no need for fear. He was the only one who could help her save Charlot.

"I know why you are here." His voice possessed the likeness of crackling fall leaves beneath her feet. The smell coming off him resembled mothballs in a closet.

Alma pushed out the words stuck in her throat. "You do?"

"Yes. I do. As I told the other, you may go in, but if you return, you cannot go back."

"I know. My sister told me all about you." Alma couldn't control the excitement in her voice.

"Then go." The creature lifted his hand, pointing a bony finger at the entrance.

She didn't ask if he was truly *Mandaamin* but darted inside to stalks deader than the creature outside. Theodore stayed on her heels. Edie had mentioned she'd gone straight to the back, so that was the direction Alma took, clutching her rifle. She ensured to unlock the safety because her weapon was loaded and ready. If anything jumped out, she just had to shoot.

Nothing jumped out at her, though.

The moonlight provided ample illumination, so she didn't have to squint. And as she walked, what unfolded became what Edie had described. The stalks were greener, the corn lush and ripe, ready to be picked.

Not a sound came from anywhere, only her gentle footsteps and the breaths from her and Theodore as she crept along the grassy floor of the maze. She continued, determined to reach the end, but the row seemed infinite. How long had her sister walked? Did it seem like forever, but was only a short journey?

She kept going.

Suddenly, before her, a wall of corn stalks turned into flickering flames, reminding her of a mirror on fire.

Oh hell, she'd found it. The very spot that would take her hopefully to Charlot to save him from death.

But what about Theodore? Would they walk into a trap? An ambush? A war?

Chapter Two: Lady in Disguise

CHARLOT HELD HIS MUSKET against him. If he turned around, he'd find many Sioux with arrows aimed at his back. Perhaps not. They were also distracted by the wall of fire he'd pushed Fire Woman through. Now she was gone.

His mind still couldn't fathom what he'd witnessed moments ago after following Thunder Bear's orders, husband to Fire Woman, a beautiful lady he'd been foolish enough to lay down his life for.

Now he'd most likely die, but he'd fight until the bitter end, taking maybe one enemy with him since he had only one round in his musket, so he must make the shot count. Pondering Fire Woman's whereabouts could wait until much later.

He whipped on his heel and aimed, firing into the group of Sioux warriors who still gaped at the spot where the wall of fire had vanished.

He hit one warrior. The big brute fell, clutching his chest.

Charlot bounded forward and jumped into the bush. He hit the ground, rolling many times to avoid the arrows that would no doubt come his way. One whizzed by his head and pierced the tree. Shouts followed.

He crawled, not daring to look up. He also didn't have time to reload his musket. Finding a spot to hide was imperative.

The Sioux suddenly fell silent, the orders in their language ceased.

Charlot didn't dare move. Something had distracted them, but what could it be? Footsteps trampled along the forest floor, followed by a whoosh through the air.

Chaos.

Absolute mayhem.

Shouts.

But he kept his head buried, praying the cover of the bush would keep him hidden from the Indians, who seemed to see through everything in the trees.

Another woosh sounded. Then a sharp point pierced his side, cutting beyond skin and muscle. The pain was so great he couldn't cry out. It sucked the breath from him, and he clutched his side. Everything went black.

ALMA HAD EXPECTED TO step into a battle. Reality set in. The only killing she'd done was animals when hunting with Grandpa. But if she didn't shoot, she risked her own life and Theodore's as she faced six Dakota sporting arrows.

Theodore growled, waiting for her command.

The Dakota didn't fire at her, though. They seemed to fire everywhere else, hollering in a language she couldn't comprehend. The fear in their eyes indicated she'd terrified them.

Maybe they assumed she was a ghost when she'd emerged through the flickering flames.

As the Dakota scattered, she tracked their moccasin footprints, but one set stood out. Grandpa had told her about the spread of the toes, and these toes weren't spread. They came from a person who walked in shoes or boots. Someone who later in life had switched to the footwear of the Indigenous people.

She followed the footprints with Theodore beside her, sniffing. She used the end of her rifle to move aside the thick brush, which was why her homeland was called *the bush* at her reserve. There was nothing to call a *forest* or *woods* about Northwestern Ontario.

The thick underbrush kept trying to snag her clothing. Clothing she longed to remove. When she left home, she'd donned an outfit for a cold Halloween night. But summer bloomed here. She could remove her jacket since she had a sweater underneath, and beneath that a tank top.

A groan came about ten feet from her, and she aimed her rifle in the direction of the sound. She moved through the many twigs and branches but didn't spot a blood trail. Whatever lay beneath the berry bush had been hit there.

Another groan.

Whoever was hurt wasn't an animal. That was the sound of a human being. Maybe one of the Dakota?

She edged in closer until she caught the moccasins sticking out, along with breeches. This wasn't a Dakota or warrior from the village under attack.

Her heart held its beat.

Had she found Charlot?

She was near the place where Charlot had shoved her sister through the dancing fire.

Theodore poked his big head around her.

She used the end of the rifle to uncover a man who fit her sister's description, drinking in his light brown hair mixed with shades of gold tied back in a ponytail. His face was the color of tanned cream. Long lashes in a rich shade of dark brown dared her to touch. A stubble of whiskers graced his pronounced chin. He wore no toque, but in such warm weather, he wouldn't be wearing the wooly head covering.

Oh geez, he was as her sister had described.

She marveled at his strong fingers clutching his side. Red stained his hand, indicating an injury of some sort.

She slung the strap of her rifle over her shoulder and knelt beside him. When she slipped her hand beneath his nose, warm breath greeted her. Relief flooded her chest. He was alive. She pushed his hand aside, revealing a broken arrow. He'd foolishly tried to detach the damned thing before passing out. Hopefully the arrowhead was made of stone.

She removed her backpack.

Charlot groaned again, still blacked out somewhere far from the pain he was probably experiencing.

She used her knife to cut away at the cloth around his wound while Theodore sniffed the air like a good boy, searching for intruders. Once she had a clear view, she worked at removing the arrow shaft. Much to her relief, it slid from him easily. Just as fast, she pressed a cloth against his wound, pushing hard to try and stop the blood flow.

"Fire Woman," he murmured.

Alma stiffened. Old resentments tried to rear forth—resentments stemming from childhood, when everyone had pushed her aside for her beautiful and dutiful sister, admired by the elders and the boys. Even parents beamed at Edie, all saying she was lovely.

For some reason, although Edie hadn't said so, the Frenchman was clearly enchanted by her older sister's beauty.

However, there wasn't time for Alma to grit her teeth over the past. She reached inside the backpack and bound Charlot's wound just as her great-grandfather had taught her. The mending would suffice until she could find a place of safety to begin stitching him. At least she stopped the blood from escaping. The Dakota would return. They may have been spooked off by her sudden appearance, but they'd come back in bigger numbers to look for the dancing flames.

She'd have to build some kind of travois to haul Charlot. Thank goodness Theodore had insisted on coming along. He could easily haul Charlot through the bush to safety, which would save her from having to lug a man bigger than her. For being regarded as such a tomboy, too bad she didn't possess a man's strength.

She quickly cut various branches and lashed them together. The blanket she'd packed in her backpack would suffice to lay over the wood. She carefully rolled Charlot onto the travois.

Once she had Theodore harnessed, she hooked him to it and they were off. To where, she wasn't sure, but Theodore would find them a safe place.

SOMEWHERE IN CHARLOT'S dream, she came to him, the woman of fire who'd captured his attention from the first time he'd spied her at the fort. A beautiful woman who'd chosen Thunder Bear over him. But he'd shown her how much he cared by risking his life for her. Maybe after knowing the *Saulteurs* for so long, he was becoming one of them.

But he had no desire to join any community. It was why he worked alone and traded alone with the *Saulteurs*. It was why he'd chosen to become a *woods runner*.

A sharp pain stabbed him in the side of his gut. He tried to roll away from whatever jabbed him. But it kept poking him, sliding in and out of his skin. He forced his eyes open while trying to sit up.

"Stay down."

A feminine voice spoke in the language of the *Saulteurs*, a language he'd learned, which enabled him to trade with the people of the woodlands.

"You are hurt," she continued.

He widened his eyes, but only black dots appeared in his vision. The voice. Fire Woman? "You are here? You did not vanish into the dancing flames?" He flopped his head against the pile of leaves again.

"My sister vanished into them."

"Sister?" Again, he forced his eyes open, even though his lids protested, demanding he close them.

"Yes, my sister."

"But..." He tried to focus, and the blurred face sharpened. Yes, the eyes belonged to Fire Woman, dark, oval-shaped, and magnificent. Thick black lashes. But the face was different. Strong bone structure with a matching jawline and nose. Almost boyish.

Wait. The young female had short hair with wispy ends that lay against her flawless bronzed skin. "You are in mourning?"

She fingered her short hair. "No."

He breathed a sigh. At first, he'd assumed she'd shorn her hair because Fire Woman had died. "She lives then?"

The woman nodded.

"Who are you?"

"Alma. I am Fire Woman's sister."

"Alma. Ah, an Anglo name." He pursed his lips.

"I am named after my great-grandmother. Both of us are."

Her voice lacked the melodic dance of Fire Woman's. Force consumed Alma's speech, each word direct, even though she whispered.

"We must be quiet," she added. "We managed to drag you far enough from the battlefield, but the Dakota could be lurking somewhere."

How strange. He attempted to rise, but common sense ordered him to stay put. "But you call them *little snakes*."

Red crept along her strong cheekbones. "Yes. The Sioux. That is what I meant."

"Where did she go then? I know your people practice..." He cleared his throat, carefully choosing his words. "The *jaasakiid* contact the spirits through the shaking tent ceremony." Something he'd never believed in and thought rather foolhardy. But after what he'd witnessed... "Is that what happened?

"Yes, in a way." She motioned at his side. "I must finish this. We can talk later."

"Later..." he murmured. "How far did you drag me? You have strong bones, but you are a woman."

She frowned. "My dog, who came with me, dragged you. However, my grandfather taught me much, trained me to become an...*Ogichidaa-kwe*. Even without my dog, I could have done so."

He arched his brow. "Then I will call you *Ashwiyaa*." It was only appropriate to think of her as Arms Oneself since she... "What is that?" He'd never seen such a weapon before. Sleeker than a musket.

"It is what I brought to come and find you."

"Your grandfather thought to arm you with such a weapon, and your dog?" He wanted to sit up and look over the long gun that was neither a pistol nor a musket.

She nodded.

"If your sister disappeared into the dancing flames, is she here then? Or did she somehow return to Montréal?"

"M-Montréal?"

"Yes. She said she comes from the east. That is where her family resides."

Her throat bobbed, and she glanced away.

"Tell me. Did one of the *jaasakiid* help them?"

"Edi—You mean Fire Woman and Thunder Bear?"

He nodded. "He gave me orders to take Fire Woman from the battle. He told me the dancing flames would appear, and I was to send her through them."

"I must finish healing you." She held up the needle.

"Yes." He let go of the side he'd been holding during their talk. "Much thanks for your assistance. When the flames appeared, the Sioux were distracted by them, even fearful...especially when Fire Woman vanished into them."

There were more questions he had, like about the woman's weapon. The dancing flames. How she suddenly appeared just as Fire Woman had left. Yes, she was being deceptive. Not dishonest. More like she did not wish to share the full truth.

But he could not blame her. The other *coureurs de bois* he met out here all had their secrets, too. This was a secretive place of mystery, the perfect area for men such as him to live. The same for the *Saulteurs*, who hid much from his kind. He'd tried to spy on the *Midewiwin,* their Grand Medicine Ceremony, from the fort at the inlet, but it was kept secret from prying eyes.

But he would learn the truth from Arms Oneself, and the whereabouts of Fire Woman. He also had to unearth what had become of Thunder Bear, a man he'd grown to respect, even think of as a friend.

First, he had to heal before journeying anywhere. The Sioux continued to roam the area. Perhaps they had even taken over the small village of the *Saulteurs* he'd been visiting before the ambush.

Chapter Three: Healer

ALMA FINISHED STITCHING up Charlot. Her gaze couldn't stop caressing his smooth skin and sleek muscles, but her conscience reminded her to focus on her mission—save the Frenchman. But she could admit why she'd come.

Crazy.

How insane to become besotted by someone she'd never met and had only heard about through her sister.

He was even more handsome than Edie had described. If in the twenty-first century, he might have his hair cut into the latest shag that would feather his square shoulders. Maybe he'd even have a short style, the kind men blow-dried forward and sleeked upward with gel, such as the celebrity Machine Gun Kelly.

No, a man like Charlot would ignore fashion and style. He came here to escape the east, where law and order prevailed.

From talking to her sister, Alma felt as if she already knew him. Maybe she even experienced a niggle of jealousy over the amount of time Edie had spent with the Frenchman. What if Charlot was in love with her? Every guy fell for her sister.

Whereas Edie walked with feminine grace, Alma stomped. Edie's voice was a melody, and hers was bold and strong.

"It takes much concentration?" Charlot had a smooth voice, the kind that slid over Alma's skin and produced goosebumps.

She could imagine how he'd sweet-talk a woman into...

Heat claimed her cheeks. She ducked her head, reaching inside the backpack. "Er, yes it does."

What would he think of the bandages she'd brought? It'd be best to use moss and make a poultice. Otherwise, she'd really give herself away. It was better to let him believe she came from the east. So she rose and went to a tree to scavenge moss and what she'd need to pack his wound.

"You are versed in the art of healing?"

"My great-grandfather is a healer. He is...uh, was teaching me."

"And your grandfather taught you the art of warfare," he seemed to muse to himself.

"Yes."

"How did they produce the flickering flames? I will confess I never believed in the, ahem, mystical ways of your people. But after witnessing what I did..." A portion of doubt mingled with his words.

The more he talked, the more his silky tone caressed Alma's skin, even while she picked moss not too far from where he lay. No guy back home had made her feel this way. Not even her good friend Jared. They were hunting buddies, both sharing a love for the outdoors. They fished together. Canoed together. Hiked together. Even gutted the animals they bagged together.

She picked up the moss and strolled back to Charlot, an outdoorsman who managed to twist her insides into goo without trying. But he belonged in the wrong century. Once she healed him, she'd have to return to the dancing flames and make her way through the maze, which would disappear once she stepped from the entrance. At least that was how Edie had explained it.

Then there was Theodore. He needed food. Yes, he could hunt on his own, always snagging a rabbit here and there.

"Mmmhmm, a thinker," Charlot whispered. "Always in your mind, yes? Much different from your sister, whose eyes said everything, as well as her lips."

The green-eyed goblin resurfaced. "Lips? You shared a kiss?"

"Perhaps you are not as quiet as I surmised." He chuckled. "You spoke your thoughts rather quickly this time."

She couldn't help narrowing her brows as she knelt beside him. To hell with making a poultice. She's used what was in the backpack. He wouldn't notice the rubbing alcohol she'd put on his wound. After picking moss, she'd have to sanitize her hands again. She reached for the bottle.

"What is that?" He squinted.

"It is nothing, just something to clean my hands."

"Clean your hands?" His eyes widened.

They must not know about germs in this century. "Yes. They are dirty from picking moss. I do not want to infect your wound."

"Why not use whiskey?" He rubbed his chin.

"I do not have any." She stuffed the bottle back into the pack. "Okay, close your eyes. It will string. It will be easier for you this way."

He didn't protest and closed his eyes.

At least he was an agreeable sort of man. It made it easier for her to use the plastic bottle containing the rubbing alcohol and cotton balls. Maybe she should have hunted down the plants. Her great-grandfather had told her that everything for healing could be found in nature. As a *mide*, he was proud to pluck medicine from Mother Earth. She'd sat many times in his *mide-wiigiwaam* listening to him and other *mideg* of various degrees recite their prayers and practice medicine.

Not that she understood everything they said and did, since she still had much to learn. She'd only started learning when she was around ten, accompanying Great-Grandpa on his journeys into the bush, and helping him mix his concoctions.

Once she finished assisting Charlot, she'd fix them something to eat.

She dabbed the cotton ball on the wound she'd stitched.

His legs kicked out, and he clenched his teeth. "*Mon Dieu*. What is that?"

"It is something I need to put on before I pack your wound with the moss."

"It stings greatly." He re-clenched his teeth.

"It will only sting for a moment."

His curled fingers uncurled, and he sank back into the travois.

"You will be fine. You are lucky the arrow did not go in any further."

"I do not recall being shot at," he supplied, eyes closed and mouth tight. "I was doing my best to crawl through the bush so they would not spy me. They were distracted when your sister vanished into the flickering flames."

"At least you stayed low." She packed the moss against the wound. "This will do. What you need is time now."

"Time?"

"For your wound to heal. I have done all that I can do." She sat back.

"*Merci*. You are a good healer." He closed his eyes tight, mouth a straight line.

"I will let you rest. Once you wake, you can eat."

"Please, do not build a fire—"

"I did not plan on building one." Did he think she was some kind of fool? "My grandpa taught me everything about the bush."

"The bush?" He tapped his cheek but never opened his eyes. "That is an interesting way of referring to this place."

"It is very thick. Underbrush everywhere. The bush."

His smile returned color to his face, producing a delightful grin, maybe a bit on the sly side, even wicked, the kind meant to tease.

She couldn't stop staring at him and even had the urge her to reach out and touch his face. But she didn't dare. When his breathing became heavy and his chest rose and fell, the little voice in her head said he was asleep, and now was the moment to explore him.

His fingers weren't long and elegant but thick and strong. Alma could imagine him gripping something tightly, like maybe her shoulders. He'd draw her in, slamming her against his lean chest, and then bring his mouth down over hers, seducing her into a kiss.

Sensual ripples gathered between her legs, and she squirmed. What would it be like to experience a true kiss? Not the kind she'd endured from a rez boy who'd attempted to claim her mouth at a local dance, the meeting of their lips turning into two left feet stepping on one another. Charlot would kiss like a man. So how did a man kiss?

Edie had mentioned Charlot was twenty-six, but he didn't seem as such in this timeline. Guys at twenty-six in her time were...well, they were still trying to become established men, at least from what she'd witnessed in town and at the rez. From what Edie had also described, Charlot behaved as if he were in his late thirties. Sure of himself. Well defined with his wants and goals. He'd been on his own for a long time. How many guys from her timeline would venture out into the great wide open? Heck, some still lived at home.

Using only her index finger, she touched the back of his hand. A jolt sizzled in her chest and sprang outward, a buzzing sensation that set off alarm bells. She drew back, her breathing grew heavy, and she shifted so there was distance between them.

She'd best set up some kind of camp while he slept. That way, when he woke, she could get him fed.

CHARLOT SENSED SOMEONE had touched him. A lady's touch. Gentle. Yet firm. Was Fire Woman here? Did she make it back through the dancing flames? What of Thunder Bear? He had to unearth if his friend was alive after the attack. As much as he longed to awake from the dream, he remained sleeping, his body needing rest.

When he opened his eyes once more, he stared into darkness and the shadow of a woman. She set food on two plates. Her sitting place struck him as strange. A bedroll, but much plusher.

"Is it from your homeland?" He used his chin to motion at the bedroll.

"Yes." She whipped her gaze elsewhere.

Another lie? Perhaps. There was much mystery about Arms Oneself, for she also sat cross-legged instead of her legs to the side as *Saulteur* women did.

"I have some food. But tomorrow I will have to hunt with Theodore." She handed over the plate.

The tin he took was cool against his fingers. "*Merci*." Beans. Some kind of jelly-like meat. Whatever she'd smoked, he'd eat. Living out in the wilds, nobody turned away food, which became scarce in the winter.

He used the fork she handed him to shovel in some of the meat. A nice taste. A bit moist. But edible. "Theodore?"

"My dog." She motioned at the gigantic animal only a few feet away.

He nodded. "Where did you come by this?" He held up a fork full of the meat he'd tasted. Preserved, yes, but not smoked.

"My grandma makes it." Again, she averted her gaze.

"Why did you come, *ma chérie*?" If not for the darkness, he'd bet he'd find color on her cheeks. This made him lightly chuckle. Ah, but that was how he was. What man could resist a lady's feminine touch? Even one with boyish looks and strong features.

She thrust out her chin. "To save you."

"To save me?" This was most curious.

"Yes. Fire Woman…" Arms Oneself coughed. "She told me when you pushed her through the dancing flames, you were left with the Sioux. Someone had to save you."

"You think I needed saving? That I am not capable of saving myself?" He wasn't sure if he should be offended or flattered. Maybe a bit of both. "I have been caring for myself out here for a long time. I would have found a way to outwit them."

"They are good trackers. I think they would have found you." Her words weren't scolding but ones of concern.

"This is why you brought the weapon and *that*?" His gaze traveled to the dog.

She nodded.

"What will you do now?"

"Once you are healed, I will return."

"Through the dancing flame?"

"Yes."

"Tell me..." He scooped up some beans. "How have your *jaasakiid* managed to create it?"

"Do you mean the dancing flames?"

"Yes."

"Uh...my...um...my great-grandfather is one." Again, she averted her gaze. "He uh...did it."

Hmm, was she lying again? "He talks to the spirits? But if I recall, you told me he is a healer and teaches you medicine. That means he is a *mide*."

"You have much to learn about our ways." She kept averting her gaze. "Some can dream and see into the future."

He rubbed his chin. "I think your great-grandfather only practices medicine." Although he wanted to sit up, he couldn't and continued to lie in a half-upright position. "As do you. I need to know about the dancing flames. I know it comes from your people, because Thunder Bear knew about it. I do not think he was shocked or surprised when Fire Woman appeared to him. She did not canoe here. She came to him the same way you came to me. If we are to be together for a while, you must be honest. Starting now."

Chapter Four: Not What You See

ALMA WASN'T SURE IF she should continue to lie or tell him the truth. But if she told him the truth, he'd never believe her. When Edie had first disclosed what had happened to her, Alma sure hadn't thought her sister had told the truth. It'd been Great-Grandpa who'd changed her mind.

"I do not think you would believe me." She toyed with her food. "When Fire Woman first told me, I did not believe it. Can we wait until we find out what happened to the people? Maybe then you will believe me."

He scratched his chin. "I always thought your people to be a superstitious lot. But the more time I spend with them, the more I find that such a mystery cannot be explained."

"That is how I felt. I am versed in my culture, but there are things I cannot explain either." The scent of the canned beans tempted her to eat. She tasted the tangy flavor mixed with tomato soup.

"You said you wanted to help me. Why, if I am a stranger?"

Because I wanted to meet you. I wanted to know the man my sister had talked about. "Fire Woman wasn't in any shape to help, but I could." She swallowed. "Her pregnancy."

"Yes, she is with child. We must find Thunder Bear. The babe will need a father."

How could she tell him that if they went to the village, they'd find Thunder Bear dead, and that he now lived on in the future? "We have to wait for you to heal."

He nodded. "Then we can pass the time. What about the moccasin game?"

Gambling. She almost laughed. The *Anishinaabeg*, even in the twenty-first century, still enjoyed gambling, whether venturing to casinos or playing bingo. "We can do that. But you must eat first." This time, she firmed her tone. He wouldn't regain his strength if he kept talking. "We will play for a short time, but you must also rest."

"It can be hard to rest when a pretty girl is tending to a man." His lopsided grin wasn't boyish but coy.

Edie had also mentioned Charlot was quite the womanizer. Would he find her attractive?

"I think any woman would keep you awake." The dry retort left her mouth before she could stop herself. She'd blame the niggle of jealousy over Charlot admiring anything with a vagina.

"No. Not any woman." He shoveled more beans into his mouth. "The lady must be pretty."

A gasp almost flew from her mouth. Did he think she was pretty? No guy had ever noticed her. "I see. Like my..." She loathed to say it. "...sister?"

He cocked a brow. "Your sister is *very* attractive." His grin almost became leering.

Alma's jealousy became a screw grinding into her spine. "Yes, everyone thinks that." Again, she couldn't contain the bite in her tone.

"Hmm... You seem bothered by your sister's attractiveness. I, too, have sisters. They face a similar situation. My older sister, who is married, is considered the fairest of the fair, with beauty beyond compare. My younger sister, though, cannot compare to Brigitte."

His words soured Alma's stomach. Edie even had the prettier name. "As I said, get some rest after you eat. I will begin cleaning up." She shoved away her plate, tempted to bash it over the Frenchman's head.

"My observation bothers you." He finished the last of his meat. "I did not mean to offend. We remain friends?"

I am every boy's friend. "We only met. I would hardly call us friends."

"But we are getting to know one another, are we not?"

"Yes. I believe so." It seemed weird speaking in a language she wasn't used to. Everything seemed a bit more formal. She understood a lot of names for the plants that Great-Grandpa had taught her, but as for the rest, that would take some getting used to.

"You are not married?"

A jolt of shock punched her in the gut. "No. Why?"

"I was simply wondering. Nothing more. Your sister surprised me by not being married, either. I should have guessed you were not. A husband would never allow his wife to travel unescorted. The land here is dangerous."

She bristled. "No man tells me what to do."

"Ah, is that why you are a warrior, hmm?" He waggled his brows. "A spirited, independent woman? To arm yourself means you are."

"I am armed because I came to rescue you."

"Rescue?" He chortled. "I do not need a woman child to rescue me. But, *merci*. I do appreciate your effort."

Edie had called him a bit smug and arrogant, but in a charming way. And he was...

"Do you really think you could have escaped the Sioux on your own? Six warriors with arrows? You only have that." She pointed at his musket.

"Everyone must load and reload."

"I do not have to reload. My gun is loaded and ready to fire several times."

"It repeats?" He rubbed his cheek. "How interesting. I do know my weapons, and such a firing weapon does not exist."

"My grandpa designed it," she lied.

"He did?"

"It belongs to him. He told me to take it with me when I informed him what I was planning on doing."

He drummed his fingers on his chin. "I must say you intrigue me. I have heard there might be female warriors, but you are the first I have met. You are nothing like your sister."

The observation stung Alma like a bee's stinger. "No, we are nothing alike. I am sorry to disappoint you."

"Disappoint?" He chuckled. "My sisters are nothing alike, either. I am not disappointed."

"Do you miss them?"

"At times." He shrugged. "But I have chosen my life. This is where I belong. I do not do well with rules. Nobody governs me."

"Is that why you are not married?"

"Marriage?" He blanched. "Marriage means more rules. You must honor your wife. Be true to her. Forsake all others. I cannot promise any woman I will be true to them. It is like asking me to eat only one berry." He laughed.

His reply nicked her heart a little. But why should she care? She was only here to rescue him, even if she had dreamed about meeting him and would probably continue pining for him once she returned home.

"What about when you grow old? Will you not miss the companionship another can bring?"

"What I need is tobacco and my pipe." He folded his arms.

"Here." She reached inside her backpack and pulled out a pipe and a pouch of tobacco.

"You indulge?" His eyes crinkled.

"No, but I was told you do. I did not think you would have tobacco and a pipe with you when you were rescuing my sister." She laid the pipe and pouch on the ground, making sure there would be no accidental touching. Touching him meant... It would be too much. She'd lose herself to the handsome Frenchman if she dared to stroke the back of his hand again.

He picked up the pipe and tobacco. "Very considerate of you. And you are correct. I left everything at the lodge where I stayed. I was visiting when the Sioux attacked. *Merci.*"

"I should clean up our meal."

"There is nowhere to clean. We are not near the lake. And the Sioux watch the lake."

"I am sure there is a pond or something nearby."

"It is dark. You should not venture off alone. The Sioux could be lurking in the shadows."

His protective nature both warmed and miffed her. Warmed that he cared enough to want her to remain put. Yet slightly annoyed because she could take care of herself and didn't need anyone to babysit her. He was worse than her parents.

"My grandpa practically raised me in the bush. I know how to take care of myself."

"This is not the east." He lit the pipe.

"I know, but..." She wouldn't argue the point. "Can I have a drag?"

"Drag?" He tilted his head and frowned.

"A puff."

"Oh. *Oui.*" He handed over the pipe.

She took it from him, making sure she only grasped the pipe's stem. Smoking with Grandpa and Great-Grandpa, along with her father and mother, had prepared her for the taste of the tobacco and the smoke that would scorch her throat. So when she inhaled, the burning sensation didn't bother her. It was rather nice to puff away without praying.

"You enjoy smoking, besides for ceremonial purposes?"

She handed over the pipe. "This is my first time for pleasure."

"Ah." He grinned. "You are a rebel, are you not? Women do not smoke from pipes."

"This one does." The drag had created a joyful spark of butterflies in her stomach.

"Fascinating." He motioned at her pack. "You came prepared. Is this something your grandfather also taught you?"

She nodded. "He shared lots with me, especially about surviving in the bush. He..." She couldn't say he *worked up the lakes*, what everyone on the rez referred to as *off the grid*. "He survived for a long time in the bush. Far up the lakes. He did so for most of his life. Kind of like you. So did my grandma."

She couldn't tell him they'd run a camp. Tourist camps didn't exist in this century.

"A lot of the Indians were hired as guides to help us explore this area at first. Is that what they did?"

"Yes, in a way, but they never came this far."

"Your father did not protest at you learning such skills?"

"No. He knows I am not one for..." What did women do during this era? "Cooking and cleaning."

"You frowned," he pointed out. "Remember, the women keep these communities running. I have great respect for what they do. Their work is hard."

"I am not belittling them, or saying what men contribute is superior. All work is important to keep a community running. I honor the women in my family and all that they do. But it has never interested me."

"When you take on a husband, he will expect you to keep the lodge, for who will?"

She'd hire a cleaner if she ever got married. But she couldn't say as much to Charlot. "I am sure I can formulate a plan of some kind."

"How old are you? Because time is growing short."

Yes, she'd be a spinster, or whatever they called unmarried women in this day and age. "Maybe I will not ever marry then."

He hiked a brow, his grin one of amusement. "I would say *who will care for you then, once you are out from the guardianship of your parents*, but I have a hunch, since you can hunt, you will manage."

Yes, manage.... She'd be on her own, back at school, working toward her BA. Existing. Trying to find a place where she fit in. "Maybe I will trap and trade the furs." Great-Grandpa had done so until he retired. The same for Grandpa before fur became taboo, and no money could be made.

"You? Remain here? I do not think it is safe unless you have a husband."

"I more than proved I can care for myself. I will take care of our camp. Tomorrow, I will bring Theodore with me, and we will hunt for breakfast. I think this is something I can do."

"It is hard work." He held out his hands, showing his creased and chaffed palms.

"There is nothing salve cannot cure. I can make myself some."

He chuckled and puffed again on his pipe.

"What is amusing?"

"You have an answer for everything."

A hint of annoyance spread across the back of her neck. Mom said the same thing. Alma swallowed. Was she behaving like a child? She was eighteen. Not a kid.

"I would not say *everything*. I simply know my capabilities. What I can do. And what I cannot do."

"And what else are you capable of? What are you not capable of, hmm?" He took another drag off the pipe.

His questions seemed to be a dare. Or maybe an innuendo of some type. Did he mean what made her heart beat faster? What made sensual flutters rise between her legs?

Chapter Five: Edge of Thorns

CHARLOT PUFFED ON THE pipe while Arms Oneself cleaned up the campsite. Wherever she moved, the dog followed—a true faithful companion. He had to admit she intrigued him. She was nothing like Fire Woman, with the exception that they shared the same eyes. The brows were different, though. Fire Woman's were slim with a beautiful arch. As for Arms Oneself, hers were thicker and more of a straight line. This gave her a serious look, especially when she frowned, making her brows slant downward.

He doubted she'd marry. A woman like Arms Oneself was too spirited, and too independent. He couldn't see any husband tolerating her views when a man needed a woman to cook and clean.

Holy matrimony was a sacred sacrament to his people. There was even a priest at another fort far from here whom he'd met twice. He did receive Holy Communion during those times after confessing his sins. But he didn't consider himself devoted to God or the Church. He was simply following how he'd been raised since his schooling came from the Jesuits back in Montréal. The same for his sisters, who'd received their teachings from the *Congrégation de Notre-Dame* at the stable school.

His father had wanted him to learn to read and write before succeeding him. He'd said knowledge was the key to success and to ensure nobody swindled his son. Knowledge also gave Charlot power over those who could not calculate figures through arithmetic.

"Did you also attend the stable school?"

Arms Oneself stopped cleaning the plates she scrubbed with damp moss. "I do not know what you mean."

Hmm, she should know of the school if she were truly from the east.

"Someone must have taught you to read and write. I assume you know how." He took his last puff of the tobacco. "You strike me as very intelligent."

"My mother taught me."

If not for the darkness, Charlot had a hunch he'd find her cheeks on the pink side. "Did you mother attend the school?"

"Yes."

She'd answer rather quickly. Too quickly.

"You should rest now. The sooner you heal, the better off we will be for safety's sake. The Sioux could still be patrolling." She kept her head down, still scrubbing the plate.

"I will rest then. I do have one question before I sleep." He pulled up the blanket.

"What is that?"

"The name of the school." He hid his grin beneath the covering.

Her back was to him, but he didn't miss the sharp intake of breath, followed by silence.

"Well?"

"I cannot recall."

Liar.

He closed his eyes. Come morning, he'd get the truth. They would not continue to speak until he learned who the sisters truly were.

THE FIRST THING ALMA did was scout the area before attempting to search for food. All she'd found was one fallen warrior, a nasty sight to see with his face to the ground, arms extended, and body frozen stiff.

She'd witnessed death many times during her hunting expeditions with Grandpa, and had even hung many a deer to bleed out. But she'd never seen human death before. Theodore had been the one to alert her to the crows and ravens, trying to pick at the fallen warrior.

She whipped her gaze away, stomach attempting to revolt. At least he hadn't been dead long enough to smell. Guilt gnawed at her conscience. Maybe she was an impetuous child, as Mom called her. Acting first and not thinking about the consequences until it was too late. How could she be, though? Hunting had taught her to plan and think of the impact, such as ensuring she never killed a mother with a child.

There was nothing she could do for the dead man. The arrow in his back said there'd probably been a misfire by one of his comrades, much to her relief. Or maybe he'd been caught in the crossfire when they'd attempted to flee the dancing flames.

She backtracked his footsteps, easing through the bush, using the end of her rifle to push aside the boughs. She found his quiver caught on a branch, which contained a good five arrows for her to use. She reached for the sack made from deer hide and slung it over her shoulder. After a few more steps, she located his bow.

In the past, among her people, warriors fashioned bows for themselves. This bow was fit for the warrior, not her. But she had to take a chance and try to use the weapon, because if she fired her rifle at something for the next meal she'd cook for Charlot, the Dakota might hear. Until she did a full scout, she had to maintain silence and hide their position.

At least the Dakota had left, but they might still be within gunshot distance. Or they might return to retrieve the fallen warrior's body for a proper burial.

She trekked back the way she came.

Because of the Dakota, she couldn't return to check on her people who'd been attacked. She'd have to take Charlot east, not west. Plus, she had to stick to her main plan—nurse him to good health so he could fight on his own.

With Theodore shadowing her heels, she finally made her way to where she'd left Charlot. The area was much different from what she was used to in the twenty-first century. But Charlot knew the bush like the back of his hand after trapping and trading here for so long. He could probably find a way to safety on his own, far from where the Dakota had attacked.

She found him resting against a tree with his hand on his side. He probably needed some type of painkiller, which she could not reveal until she decided if she should tell him the full truth. The right plants for healing should be around here somewhere, though.

"How are you?" She set the quiver against a rock, along with the bow.

"Where did you find those?" He stared at their new weapons.

"With a fallen warrior." She knelt beside him to check his wound.

"You killed him?"

Was he kidding? This may be the eighteenth century, but she was from the twenty-first, where people didn't go around shooting any ol' body. "No. I found him dead with an arrow in his back. He must have received the death wound when they were fleeing the dancing flames."

"The dancing flames..." He motioned at the pack. "Hand me more tobacco, please."

Alma reached into the backpack.

"Did you go through his belongings? He might have been carrying something in his bag."

She didn't think to check, but she should have since the men of her band used bandolier bags. "I can go back and look." She held out the tobacco.

He took the cloth baggie.

For the briefest moment, their fingers touched, which sent an electrical current that shot up Alma's arm. She snatched away her hand, settling on her haunches. The warmth of his flesh created hot coals in her belly.

He stuffed the pipe. "If you go back, they might be there to retrieve his body. It is best to let it go."

"I will go back now. Before they return. It is early. The sun has only just risen."

He knitted his brows. "I guess I should have saved my words, for you are determined to do whatever you wish, no matter the consequences."

He sounded just like Mom and Edie.

Alma thrust out her chin. "Why do you insist on telling me what to do?"

"Because I have lived out here for a long time. I am aware of my surroundings and what can happen. Are you?"

Her face heated.

"You say you are a warrior... A warrior proceeds with caution."

She bit back the snark ready to leave her mouth. This wasn't her mom she was arguing with, but a man she'd dreamt about. "Very well. I will not retrieve his belongings."

"I did not say that you cannot. I said—"

"I did not ask for your permission," she snapped, yearning to cover her ears. The man nagged worse than her parents. "I said I will not go back. Maybe after a couple of days it will be safe. Then I can retrieve his belongings...if they do not collect his body and he is still there."

He sighed. "*Mon Dieu*. I pity the man who marries you."

His insult cut straight to her heart. "What do you mean?" He might as well have slapped her. After dreaming about this man, thinking about him, he wasn't what she'd hoped he'd be. The man was arrogant... Cocky... A total jerk.

"No wonder Edie chose Adrian." She hissed the words in English before she could take them back.

"What is this? Who do you speak about?"

"Never mind." She stood. "I am going to collect more firewood."

"No. You explain yourself, for I think you insulted me somehow, but you used mysterious words."

There he goes bossing again. Fine. He wanted to know the truth...she'd give him the truth. "No wonder my sister chose Thunder Bear over you. She is wise, and *Anishinaabe-kweg* choose wisely. You may be handsome. You may be able to offer riches and trinkets, but your personality stinks." She sniffed the air. "It stinks like the ass of a skunk."

He blanched, straightening, but winced and pressed his hand to his side. "You dare to insult me? Listen, little one. I did not ask you to rescue me. You did this of your own accord." He wagged his finger. "If you think I will sit here and take your insults, think again. Your parents have spoiled you. They should have spanked your bottom while you were still young enough to receive a spanking."

She should have found his attack offensive, but the word *spanking* had a different effect by producing shivers down her spine and those darn sensual trembles between her legs. She raised her chin. "My parents would never touch me that way. I pity you if yours took a paddle to your backside."

"The way to raise children is with a firm hand. My father used a firm hand. You do not see me offending others, as you do."

"You brought this on yourself when you said you pity the man who marries me. Maybe I have no desire to marry? There are many women who do not marry."

"Yes." He snickered. "Maybe because no man wishes to marry them."

"Maybe they *choose* not to marry."

"I do not know of any woman who would choose not to marry." He coated each word with pure smugness.

Anger unfurled in her chest. "I will be one of those who choose not to marry. And I know a couple of women who—"

"Have you asked them why?"

The way he kept speaking in his know-it-all tone became an itch under her skin, and she gasped. "I will do no such thing. That is personal."

"Personal or not, I believe they did not choose to remain single."

"What is wrong with you?" This was not the man she'd envisioned saving.

"Wrong with me?" Laughter tinged his question.

"Yes. Why are you such an..." She couldn't say asshole, unsure if the insult existed in this period. And saying so in Ojibway did not sound correct, for the interpretation stank worse than a skunk. "Why are you so difficult?"

"Difficult? I am not the difficult one. You are. You choose to make everything difficult. I am sitting here, injured, while you continue to antagonize me. All I am doing is trying to keep you safe since you put no thought into the impact your actions will produce."

He was no better than her older brothers, Edie, and her parents. Always belittling her. Always telling her what to do. How she loathed being the youngest in the family.

"Did you even think about how you will return once I am healed?"

"I will return to the dancing flames."

"What if they do not appear?"

A humongous wave of shock slapped Alma across the face. She almost stumbled.

Edie had found her way back. The dancing flames had reappeared when Edie needed to return at such a crucial time.

Alma almost threw up her hands in frustration. Why had she assumed the flames would do the same for her? What if they didn't appear? What if she became stuck here with the biggest jerk who'd ever walked the earth? A rascal of a man, too handsome for his own good, but also an arrogant shmuck.

What if she could never go back?

Chapter Six: The Message

"AHA." THE FAMILIAR smug smile spread across Charlot's face. "You did not think of how you could return, did you? Do not lie. Your eyes say I speak what is in your thoughts."

Alma whipped her gaze away. He was right. Fear almost struck her down like a lightning strike. The thought of never getting home, of not seeing her family again, especially her great-grandparents and grandparents, nearly returned her to a moment of being a little girl, ready to flop against a tree and cry over her stupid mistake.

Wait, she could not... would not cry. That was what eighteen-year-olds did in the twenty-first century. In the eighteenth century, she was considered a full-grown woman, capable of raising a family and being responsible for a lodge. She might even have her first child already.

"I suppose I am to return you back east?"

If she kept hearing him speaking in his smug voice, she'd serve him up skunk for supper. "I am perfectly capable of returning east on my own."

Plus, she couldn't have him take her to Montréal, because there was nothing to return to.

"Do not despair, *mademoiselle*. I will see you safely back east."

"Do I look like I am upset?" She threw out her hands. "I am fine. I got myself here, therefore I can get myself back."

"It seems we will be spending a lot of time together. Perhaps you can now tell me the truth." He used a tinder box he'd removed from his shirt to light his pipe. "How about you prepare us some tea?"

"That means we will have to start a fire. What if the Sioux smell it?"

"We do not need a full fire. A few coals. Nothing more."

"They might smell that too. A fire is a fire." She toyed with her fingers, unable to stop thinking about being trapped here. "Maybe they smell your pipe."

"Well?"

She glanced up.

"Are you going to tell me the truth. Do you really think I have not studied your weapon? Do you think I have not noticed your bedroll?"

She followed his gaze, which rested on the zipper she tried to hide.

"I heard it last night. I heard a funny noise before you climbed inside. Then I heard it make the same noise when you fastened it."

"You will not believe me."

"Let me be the judge." He'd softened his voice. Even his green eyes had softened.

Loneliness consumed her like a blanket. She plopped on the sleeping bag. "*Mandaamin* is the corn spirit of my people."

"I am aware of him. Your people sing his praise for bringing corn to them. They hold a feast in the fall when the corn is ripe and ready to eat."

"Are you aware of corn mazes?"

He squinted.

Great. He wasn't.

"I am aware they plant the seeds in a hole and create a mound around it. They call it *Miijinimaaganag*, for three sisters are involved. They plant the corn and beans in the same hills, then plant the squash between the rows. It is companion planting, like sisters are companions. They help the other grow. Does not your sister help you grow?" he asked.

Alma glanced down. Edie had tried many times to help her, but she'd ignored her sister's pleas. All because of envy, wishing she could be as stunning and compassionate. "I suppose I could listen to Fire Woman more often."

Charlot arched a brow. "You are a rebellious one. Strong-spirited. No wonder you are a warrior."

Alma's skin warmed. That was the first true compliment he'd give her, instead of always speaking in his upbraiding tone. And it came because she'd been honest with him.

"Being a warrior means you need a strong spirit. But sometimes our strength can turn to stubbornness. For you are also stubborn," he added.

She flinched, but this time she wasn't offended because he meant well. "A maze is hard to explain. Let me try using these sticks." She began forming a maze with them. "See what I am making? Think of it as enormous. A gigantic maze you can get lost in."

He rubbed his chin and narrowed his eyes, staring at the stick maze she'd created on the ground. "Yes. I think I understand, but I am having a hard time visualizing it."

"Where I come from, we have corn fields, like you do. You know, you plant one row, then another, then another."

"Yes."

At least she had gotten something right. "This maze had paths leading in all kinds of different directions. When Fire Woman saw it, something that had never been in our area before, she stopped to investigate why there was a maze instead of corn field."

He kept rubbing his chin, staring at the sticks made into a maze, nodding.

"*Mandaamin* was there. He was guarding this corn maze." She waited for Charlot to scoff, but he didn't, so she continued. "He used the thunderbirds to summon her there, as if he'd been waiting." She grabbed one of the sticks from the maze to toy with. "When she approached him, he told her whatever she wished for, it would come true. She was not sure if she should proceed, but he told her to go inside."

She licked her lips. "My sister is, well, was obsessed with our ancestors. It was what she was studying in school before she came upon the corn maze. So when she wished, she wished to see our ancestors."

"Ancestors?" He ceased staring at the sticks and gazed at her with a frown.

"I told you. It is hard to explain. Even I did not believe her tale when she first told me. It was my great-grandfather who convinced me she spoke the truth."

He continued to stare.

Her hands shook, so she tossed aside the twig. "When she was inside this maze, the dancing flames appeared. All she had to do was step through them, and she came here."

"Here. The same spot where she left?"

She nodded. "Thunder Bear was waiting for her. He told her he had been waiting a long time for her to appear."

"He believed her?"

"He saw it during his vision quest. He knew *Gitche Manidoo* was sending her to him, and for him to be patient."

"He was convinced your creator, this great spirit being of your people, sent Fire Woman to him?"

"Yes."

"When the Sioux attacked, how did he know the dancing flames would appear?" he asked.

"He did not reveal all his vision, because he could not. None of us can. He only knew he could not get her there since he had to help the people of his village, so he asked you to take her there."

"Yes, of course I helped him. I have much respect for him. I also respect their marriage."

"They are married and safe where they are. They had a child. A boy." Her lower lip trembled. "Charlot."

His eyes widened. "*Mon Dieu.* They named the babe after me?"

"Yes. When you pushed Fire Woman through the dancing flames, she thought she would never see you again. She even feared you would perish at the hands of the Sioux. To honor all you did for them, they named their child after you."

"You have seen this child?"

"Of course. I am his auntie. I love him very much. He is a good baby."

"So you believed I would die, and that is why you sought out this maze and *Mandaamin*?"

She nodded. "I spent..." How could she tell him she'd spent a year going to the place where Edie had said the maze was located, all for naught until Halloween?

"*Mandaamin* grants wishes, and he granted my wish. I told the corn spirit I wanted to come back here and save you."

"Tell me more about Fire Woman's wish. She disappeared back to the place where you came from."

"She wished to meet her ancestors and even live as them. My sister..." Alma licked her lips. "She was obsessed with them. Her studies in school were on them. She knows more about this time period than I do."

He held up his finger. "That is what I am seeking. You said *time period.* What do you mean exactly?"

She lowered her head. "This is where you will not believe me." She forced her gaze upward to meet his intense stare, his green eyes almost delving inside of her. "When she went into the flickering flames, it took her back to the corn maze. And the corn maze is far ahead in time. Very far."

His slim jaw slackened.

"It is how I have this." She held up part of the sleeping bag she sat on. "And that." She nodded at her rifle. "And these." She reached inside her pack and withdrew the bottle of ibuprofen. "These will help with your pain." She opened the bottle and held out the pills.

"You are telling me that Fire Woman disappeared back to the maze, and it is somewhere in the future?" His jaw tightened, his eyes burning with accusation.

"I knew you would not believe me. I had no intention of telling you anything. I only planned on helping you. There is also no reason to check on the people in the village. They are not there. What is left of them fled. As I said, Fire Woman is happily married to Thunder Bear because he is alive and well with her in the future."

"I cannot believe it." But he eyed her rifle. "And I will not believe it."

NIGHT HAD FALLEN, AND Charlot lay on his back, staring upward, but he couldn't quite see the stars through the forest's canopy.

If he believed Arms Oneself's tale, he might as well admit to being madder than she was. He rubbed his brow. Her shorn hair indicated a fever of some sort. Perhaps she was ill and hallucinating. Or maybe she was a lunatic. If she'd lied to him from the start, she would have to lie again. Yes, the *Saulteurs* were mystical people, greatly influenced by the supernatural. Everything they believed started in the spirit world with them.

But he was not a believer in such nonsense. To believe went against everything he knew.

He puffed on the pipe, grateful she'd at least packed tobacco before appearing from the dancing flames.

"What am I to believe?" he whispered to himself.

He glanced at Arms Oneself, cradling her firearm with her faithful dog curled up beside her. How could a *Saulteur* family acquire such a weapon anyway? The same for her bedroll, with the funny metal teeth lined together that she used to open and close the sleeping contraption.

He dreaded what stared him in the face, almost like observing his reflection in a still pond. Arms Oneself could be telling the truth. There was no other explanation. What annoyed him was that if he hadn't persisted, and if he hadn't been injured, she never would've told him about her secret—the same secret she shared with Fire Woman. Even Thunder Bear knew the truth.

The savvy warrior hadn't bothered to second-guess the story Fire Woman had spun.

Charlot took another puff from the pipe. It was imperative that they head for the village once he recovered. If Thunder Bear was present, he could speak to him.

Wait, Arms Oneself said they wouldn't find the warrior there. A trick? Something she'd conjured up to keep more of her secret hidden. He would go there, no matter what she said.

If he wanted to learn the full truth and expose the last of her secrets, what was left of the Indians could reveal much to him.

He glanced back over to where Arms Oneself slept. There had to be more to why she risked so much than wanting to save him. If she was as cunning in the forest as she appeared to be, instinct would have told her he didn't need her help, and she would've remained from whence she had come.

He'd find a way to learn her true intentions.

He could even consider seducing her to find out what he needed to know.

He balked.

Seduce?

He'd never thought twice about seducing a maiden.

Yet, he wasn't sure what to make of her.

She didn't possess the beauty of her sister.

And she was stubborn.

Perhaps he should take the seduction route. If she could play these silly female games with him, he could play games with her, too.

Chapter Seven: Silk and Steel

THE SCENT OF FIRE WOKE Alma. She scrambled to sit up. What the heck was Charlot doing? No, he didn't have an all-out fire going, but the burning coals could alert someone to their presence.

"What are you doing?" She couldn't help the scolding in her question.

"What does it look like I am doing? I am making myself some tea."

"You are supposed to remain in your bedroll." She wormed out of her sleeping bag and tromped over to where he squatted, poking at the coals.

"I am sure the Sioux have left."

"What if they are making camp at the village? What if they are torturing the captives?" She set her hands on her hips. "I did not come back to rescue you only to have to rescue you again."

"We are far enough from where the flickering flames appeared."

"They will smell it. The animals taught them. They are—" Her face heated. "*Sauvage*?"

She gasped. "That word was used enough in the—" She covered her mouth since it was what the nuns had called Great-Grandpa and the other children who'd been forced to attend the Indian Residential Schools.

Closing her eyes, she called on everything to not toss something at Charlot. But he was only behaving like a *coureur de bois* according to his time. Plus, Great-Grandpa had said the word was interpreted differently by the nuns. They hadn't literally called the kids a bunch of heathen savages as the English government had done. The nuns had meant wild. But not *animal* wild. Instead, they used it for those who did not follow the government's rules, who did not honor God, and had their own way of living off the land.

Wild?

Yes.

That word was the closet interpretation the French nuns could come up with.

Edie had said all languages did not translate properly. The French could have even seen them as unspoiled, another translation for *sauvage*, meaning pure and untainted. Maybe even uncorrupted by the European rules and regulations. After all, the French had been their allies. Edie had said the *Anishinaabeg* had possessed great respect for the French king.

"Did I say something to offend?" He held up the other cup for her.

"No." She shook her head. "Thank you." She took the cup from him.

Again, their fingers brushed. The hot electricity shot up her arm, heating her skin. As aggravating as he was, she loathed even more the damned attraction crackling between them. Had she been in love with him all along?

Impossible.

Nobody could fall in love without meeting the person.

And now that she'd met him, he could... Go to hell? No, she didn't want him to end up there.

"Are you well?" His green eyes studied her, stroking her face, even touching her cheek.

She clutched the tin cup, which warmed her hands. "Yes. I am fine. I was thinking..."

"Oh? Are you thinking about where you truly come from?" He cocked a brow.

Not that again. Would he ever leave it alone? Doubtful.

"I was thinking about something else, like our first meal of the day. I need to try out the bow and arrow."

"It is not fashioned for you. The aim could be well off."

"It does not matter. I will have to try since we need to eat."

"*Oui*. But maybe now that I am feeling stronger, we could move our camp toward one of the smaller lakes."

"Smaller lakes?" She hadn't roamed the backwoods of Morson in her century.

He used his chin to indicate eastward. "It will not take long."

"But you are injured." Frustration gathered in her chest because he was bossing again.

"I am capable of walking. We cannot walk fast, but I am not lame."

"Very well." She tapped her fingers against the cup. "We can fish."

"You said your grandfather taught you everything to survive out here. Do you know how? Hunting would prove useless. The animals are not fattened up during this season. It is why your people fish *esturgeon*."

Heat flared again, this time on her face. "Yes. I know." She wasn't stupid. Hunting always occurred in the fall.

"Do not take offense." He held up his hands in self-defense. "I was merely asking if you know how to fish. I do not wish to assume. Nothing more."

She had to stop snapping at him. He was making her out to be a bitch with the way she kept jumping at his replies. "Very well. You can lead us. We will need to pack up."

"Yes. That is what one does when they move locations." He chuckled.

Geez, there he was, deliberately annoying her again. "I do not think I need that explained to me." She didn't mean to bark, but around him, communicating like an ornery rez dog came easy. Turning her back to him while packing was the best way to keep her temper in check. "Let me ready everything. Then we can be on our way. Theodore is not around. He must have gone to catch food."

"Absolutely. But there is no rush. Did you not want to finish your drink first?"

"No." Drinking meant sitting, which led to talking, and having a conversation with him led to bickering. "I will get everything ready. Finish your pipe."

"Very well."

As she rolled up her sleeping bag, the aroma of burning tobacco reached her nostrils. Part of her wished to ask for another drag, but the other part ignored the temptation of the scent, reminding her she brought the tobacco for him specifically.

Once she finished, she stood, sliding her arms through the straps of the backpack. She grabbed her rifle.

She turned.

Charlot leaned on a branch that served as a cane. He held his musket in his free hand.

"Is that loaded?"

"Of course."

"Really?" She couldn't help her curiosity about how the contraption worked. But she decided to save her questions until they reached the small lake he'd mentioned, where they could catch some food. Maybe even find some privacy to let down their guards instead of sleeping with one eye open, as she'd done the previous night, while feeling him staring at her.

Just then, Theodore bounded through the bush. He wagged his tail, licking his chops, which meant he had indeed hunted something for himself.

"We are off." Charlot stuck the branch in the ground and pointed in the direction with the musket in his free hand.

He led the way, having to push aside the thick pine boughs.

Alma used the tip of her gun to stop the branches from slapping her in the face while following his path. Since Charlot hobbled, she found herself wondering what his true gait was like. A strut? Probably. He reeked of confidence, and a confident man had an assured gait.

"You said the musket only allows you one shot, right?"

Charlot nodded. He craned his neck, whispering, "Quiet."

Alma bordered on slapping her own face for thinking herself an outdoorswoman when she had to be reminded of the golden rule while traversing through the forest. Charlot was listening, and even Theodore had perked his ears, while dumb her was too busy staring at Charlot's backside, admiring his slim physique with taut muscles, and how he stealthily prowled the bush, even while injured.

She wasn't sure how long they walked, but the sun in the sky indicated it was almost noon. The croaking of frogs alerted her to a nearby pond or water source.

The lake.

She continued to follow Charlot until the bush opened to Eden.

Alma sighed. A bath sounded heavenly. She could scrub off the grime and let the soothing water untie her taut muscles.

"Here we are," he said, motioning at the water, as if she couldn't see the lake.

She wouldn't offer a rebuttal of the obvious but chalk up his comment to part of his personality. "It looks refreshing."

"Yes. A nice cool drink." He hobbled to the rocky shoreline since there was no beach, only tons of spruce trees and rocks.

A warning sat on the tip of her tongue, but she swallowed the words, or he'd become annoyed, since that was what they seemed to do best with each other.

"Let me get the cups." She gladly let the pack fall and set down her rifle.

Thedore bounded for the water. He submerged himself, paddling about.

Charlot knelt on a rock, dipping his hand into the water.

Again, Alma shoved aside her irritation since the man never had an ear out for what she had to say. She withdrew a cup and meandered to the rocks, careful to steer clear of him, or someone might end up face-first in the lake.

She dipped her cup. When the cold liquid entered her mouth, excitement danced on her taste buds. Clean, refreshing, and cool. No need for filtering.

This place was as unsullied and innocent as Edie had mentioned.

Alma rested on her haunches, careful to keep her balance so she didn't fall in. From the corner of her eye, she spied Charlot continuing to cup water into his hands, slurping up the tasty refreshment. Some dribbled down his chin and onto his linen shirt.

She glanced away. In a day or two, he'd be well enough to survive on his own. Then she'd attempt to return home, making her way back to where she'd come through the flickering flames.

As she looked around the area, she finally understood why her sister hadn't wanted to return. Talk about peaceful, though part of her craved a bag of potato chips and her iPhone. But this was like hunting with Grandpa—going out into the bush for a few days. However, after a few nights in the tent, she'd yearn for social media and to check the news on her latest rock group. Then there was her warm bed to snuggle in, along with opening the cupboard to grab her favorite cereal and digging around in the fridge for some milk to pour over her Corn Flakes.

"By the way you are staring at the water, do you wish to bathe?" Charlot straightened, leaning on his stick while holding his side. His shirt stuck to his chest where he'd dribbled water.

She wasn't about to get naked in front of him, even though the annoying heat slithered across her skin, and Theodore's splashes tempted her to follow her dog into the refreshing haven. "I will. But first, I will get us some fish."

He nodded and made his way to where she'd left her pack.

She'd require her blade to fashion a sharp stick to spear the fish since she didn't have netting. Hopefully, she would be successful, otherwise she'd have Charlot's snide remarks to deal with, or worse, rely on him to catch breakfast.

She shuffled to where he sat, already having lit his pipe. He'd run out of tobacco soon, which meant a trip to the fort since there were no *Anishinaabeg* to trade with after the Sioux massacre.

"You have what you need?" He motioned at the backpack.

"Yes." She dug inside and withdrew the knife.

"I must say, I am most interested in your weapon." He glanced at the rifle.

"If we have time, I can show you how to use it, as long as you show me how to use yours." She pointed at his musket.

He grinned. "I can teach you."

"Deal."

"Deal?" He quirked his brow.

"It means I am in agreement and will teach you if you teach me." She hoped she interpreted the words properly in the language of her people.

"Ah, so much in such a small word." He nodded at her hunting knife. "That is most interesting."

"My grandfather gave it to me." She straightened. Being too close to him and his natural scent of leather and outdoors was too much for her senses. "Can you start a fire?"

"I thought you were against a fire." He chuckled.

She gritted her teeth. "I think we are far enough away to safely start one now."

"But you do not know what else lurks out here."

She almost tossed the knife...at him. "Just start a fire. I should not be long."

"May I observe?"

No. "If you wish, but a fire would be nice."

"Very well." He also stood, still holding his pipe.

She tried her best not to storm to the rocky shoreline, but his darned footsteps on the rocks indicated he was following her.

Great. He planned on watching. If she didn't catch any fish, she'd probably end up poking his eyes out with her knife.

Chapter Eight: White Flag

CHARLOT STUCK THE END of the pipe in his mouth as Arms Oneself sharpened a stick to use for fishing. This would be most interesting since the young lady considered herself made for this wild, untamed land. A woman born and raised back east, as her older sister had claimed, who relied on stores for food.

He could be wrong, though. Perhaps her grandfather did leave the town to venture out into the interior to hunt and fish. Many did. Starting with his own father, whose love of it had inspired Charlot to venture further inland to try his hand at fur trading.

Fire Woman had only said she'd come from back east. She never specified if she belonged to an Indian settlement. He rubbed his chin. They must not have, because the raven-haired beauty had struggled enormously to live out here. He'd watched her struggle, starting with her command of the canoe. But she'd acquired the skill and had been eager to learn the ways of her people.

Which meant the girls had been raised in Montréal. He'd bet his new pipe on it. Unless Arms Oneself spoke the truth and came from some place far in the future. *Impossible.* Could he believe she'd emerged through the dancing flames? Yes. He had no choice because he'd witnessed Fire Woman disappearing in them when he'd pushed her into the strange phenomenon. But as for Arms Oneself? He'd been injured, hiding in the brush, unable to witness anything.

From his position on the flat rock, he watched as Arms Oneself removed her heavy boots. They had thick heels he hadn't seen before, material he'd never touched. The laces weren't from fabric he'd seen before. Even her breeches were strange, going all the way down to her ankles. When she rolled them up, she exposed short stockings that ended mid-calf. Hmm…how did they stay up since she hadn't tied them off with a garter?

Mon Dieu, he had no choice but to believe Arms Oneself.

He rubbed his forehead.

Non. He could not. If he did, he'd be considered mad, laughed at by other fur traders, ridiculed by anyone who heard about his tale. A man of his knowledge of the woodlands would never allow himself to believe such nonsense.

Yes, he could admit the *Saulteurs* possessed some magic, but to travel from a different time?

Yet most women residing in Montréal wouldn't dare show their ankles in front of a man, much less don breeches. Even the maidens out here wore dresses, and in the winter slipped on leggings to wear underneath since they did not have thick, quilted petticoats to keep them warm. They also used high-sided moccasins to protect their legs from chills.

After living out here for so long, he dressed the same. Leggings. High-sided moccasins. A fur cap. A woolen capote. Thick fur from an animal he'd trapped. Breeches made of canvas for better drying, since skins took a long time to dry when laid out in front of the fire. Linen shirts in the summer, such as what he was currently wearing.

His clothing was still fresh, except for where he was injured, because a maiden had washed everything while he visited his *Saulteur* friends before the attack. The sorrow in his heart forced him to bow his head. Gone. Probably all of them. If not for saving Fire Woman, he too, would have perished defending the village.

He sucked harder on the pipe just as Arms Oneself waded into the water with her spear.

"I concede." He had no choice but to accept the facts staring him in the face. But the niggle of doubt resurfaced because the tale seemed impossible, much like old folklore back in France about ghosts and other apparitions.

"Concede what?" She took careful aim, staring into the water.

"I have no choice but to believe your story." He used the stick to stand. At least his left side didn't ache as much. "That somehow one of your *jaasakiid* sent you through the dancing flames."

"You should. Thunder Bear believed Fire Woman. He was the one who urged her to become one with this land." She jabbed the spear straight into the water, stabbing at something.

"But I do not believe in magic." Time travel was impossible.

"It is not magic. It is the power of the *manidoog*." She craned her neck, her stare scolding.

Ah yes, the spirits, the all-powerful beings the *jaasakiid* revered, and to whom the people worshiped at the grand medicine ceremony, where they begged for healthy, good lives.

"It is said Fire Woman came dressed as a maiden, yet you did not think to dress as one." He removed his moccasins and stockings. Using the stick, he also waded into the water, which felt refreshing on his bare skin.

"I did not think I would be here very long." Again, she took aim, having missed the first time.

"You thought to injure or kill the Sioux with your weapon and then flee into the dancing flames, did you not?"

She nodded, gazing up at him. "Yes. Though I did not arrive at the right time. My sister said she saw you turning to fight them when the vision in the flames disappeared."

He eased the spear from her hand. "Let me help." He didn't miss her sour expression. "If we wait on you, we will go hungry."

She harumphed and folded her arms. "Why do you always do that?"

"Do what?" He aimed at the *truite* moving around him, careful to keep still. "Insult me."

"I do not insult you. I am merely stating the obvious." When the fish paused, he jabbed the spear, but made sure to aim it slightly ahead of the green-skinned beauty. As the creature moved forward, the end of the spear pierced it.

He pulled up the spear, holding the end out to Arms Oneself to take the fish from the sharp tip. "Our first meal has arrived. I will catch two more for us."

Her expression looked as though she had eaten rancid food. "Very well. You are a capable man at catching fish. I concede."

"Defeat? You mean?" He couldn't help but laugh. She was like a pouting little girl. How sweet.

"Yes, defeat." She thrust her chin forward. "But do not think you can best me at everything."

"Why must you always challenge everything I do?" He again eyed the next fish swimming around them.

"Because I wouldn't be Arms Oneself if I did not. I am a warrior, and a warrior does not like to lose."

"Many do lose. It is why they honor their medicine bundles when going into battle. It is also why they seek out the *mideg* for blessings and the *jaasakiid* to foresee how they will fare. Do not think they put all their stock in themselves. That is where we differ. We rely on ourselves. Your men rely on the spirits and medicine."

"If not for your weapons, they would have defeated you." Her gaze traveled to his musket.

"Is this why your people like to arm themselves with our weapons?"

"What choice do they have?" She shrugged.

"You promised to teach me how to use yours." He speared another fish.

"If you teach me how to use yours."

"As you like to say—deal." He offered her the tip of the spear.

She removed the *truite*. "Very well. It is what we can do after we eat. I will start cooking and you can get us three more. I am famished, and Thedore needs to eat."

"A maiden with a healthy appetite. You are wise to eat as much as you can, for one never knows when they will have their next meal out here. As for your dog, I will feed him."

"It is how the animals eat, do they not?" There was a wink to her words as she slyly grinned. "And the animals are the teachers of my people." She turned.

For some reason, he couldn't help looking at her backside this time, although he hadn't before. She was slim in the hips, not rounded for growing babies in her womb, and he couldn't help admiring her figure.

She was made to be out here, hunting and fishing. For a man on his own, she'd make a wonderful companion, capable of looking after herself while also aiding in trapping furs, hunting animals, and building canoes, shelters, and everything else required to survive within the interior.

Hmm, the more time he spent with her, the more he noticed her wonderful attributes instead of the spoiled young lady who wanted her way.

"Well?" Her question held a hint of confusion.

He gaped at the spear, chuckling at his lack of concentration because he'd been too busy thinking about her.

"One moment." He cleared his throat and prepared to catch another fish.

Under her sharp eye, his concentration failed slightly, since he kept sneaking peeks her way. When she folded her arms and tapped her foot, he got down to business, refusing to play a fool. Not until she left to prepare their meal did he finally spear three more fish. He carried his catch to where she sat, having gotten a fire going.

"Do you wish to eat the eyes?" Yes, he'd offer her what he found the *Saulteurs* savored.

The look on her face said he'd offered her his toenails to dine on.

"You do not wish to eat them? Your people say they are a delicacy and most nutritious."

"I will…" She kept staring at the fish. "I will pass. But thank you for offering. It is most kind."

Hmm, she thought to thank him, and even compliment his generosity. Perhaps there was more to her than what he'd assumed. He hunkered down beside her.

She took the fish and produced a knife, one he wasn't familiar with, but the blade appeared created for filleting.

"You are going to skin the fish?"

She nodded.

The *Saulteurs* enjoyed everything from animals. Perhaps she had something in mind for the skin. As for the bones, she'd save those for needles, although most were trading for the ones at the fort.

After she filleted the fish, she used the oil from the skin to rub on the rocks where she'd cook their meal. She'd professed to be a woman made for the outdoors, and she was more than proving she did belong out here. Her grandfather had taught her well.

Once she cooked the fish, she fed the dog first, which astonished him since the animal should eat last. How strange, and maybe a bit insulting. She then handed him one of the two tin plates.

He bit into the meal, choosing to forego reprimanding her since that would produce another of their discussions when his growing belly demanded food. The *truite* lacked spice, but out here, he did not complain. Any meal was a good meal. "Delicious."

"I am glad you like it. I did not bring any seasonings, but I am used to it. Grandpa taught me to make do with what I have."

"He is a wise man. Come winter, I have seen people eat their moccasins and bark."

Her eyes widened. "Fire Woman told me. She also said you and your father had to."

"*Oui*. We faced some lean times when he took me out as a boy. But I do not regret learning such a lesson. One cannot take anything for granted out here."

"No, you cannot."

She agreed with him for once? His grin came easily.

"What?"

"We are agreeing."

"I can be agreeable." Amusement lurked in her eyes—her first truly refreshing smile that made her dark, jeweled eyes sparkle and created an attractiveness about her.

Yes, if he looked hard at her features, her square jawline suited her big, bright eyes. The same for her shorn hair with the wisps lying against her smooth skin. She might not possess her sister's stunning beauty, but Arms Oneself had a strong, long nose to match her physical strength. A prominent chin that complemented her stubbornness. And an intense stare to match her determination.

"What?" Pink flecked her cheeks, and she rubbed her face as if to wipe away some kid of imaginary dirt.

"I am simply enjoying dining with a beautiful young lady."

Her eyes widened. "What?"

"I cannot compliment you? Nobody has told you so before?"

She glanced away.

Maybe nobody had. Perhaps she fell into the background when standing beside her sister. Yes, she would. If Fire Woman and Arms Oneself had appeared to him at the same time, he would've noticed Fire Woman first, and of course, would've given the stunning beauty his full attention. With Arms Oneself, a man had to look closely, taking a moment to reflect on her physical attributes, which became more prominent the longer one got to know her.

His side ached after fishing. Once he ate, he sat back to ease the pain.

Concern reflected in her dark eyes. "You are still sore."

He nodded. "A bit of rest will help. Do not worry. I will take you to where the dancing flames are. Give me two sunrises."

"Two sunrises."

"Yes. Two. Then you can return from whence you came."

Chapter Nine: Musket & Rifle

"YES, I GUESS THAT IS what we will do." Alma swallowed. Something resembling a lump grew in her throat, which was stupid, because she'd only met the man. Then why were tears attempting to form in her eyes? Why was she hoping she could stay a bit longer? The disappointment in her chest grew from the size of a pea to a boulder.

This man, who annoyed the hell out of her, who'd failed to be who she'd dreamed about, this arrogant shmuck who somehow possessed a heart of gold he kept hidden within him, was about to make her cry. And he didn't deserve tears.

Maybe his lack of reciprocation of her feelings was the cause. She was Edie's little sister to him, and nothing more.

"I should clean up." She gathered their plates. "Get some rest." She stood. At least she had the lake where she could wash the tins she'd always used with Grandpa whenever they'd gone camping.

"*Ashwiyaa...*"

Hearing the name he'd gifted her on his tongue almost melted the icicles surrounding her heart. She remained stiff but pivoted to face him.

Charlot stared, lips parted, as if readying to say more, but then, "Yes, clean up the plates. Thank you for cooking the meal."

"Thank you for catching our fish." She turned, shoulders slumped, and headed for the small lake. Getting clean was a must. Once she finished washing the minimal dishes, she'd scrub herself.

She knelt at the rock. There was no sand to use. How would she... Wait. Grandpa had said to use the leftover ashes in the campfire.

She peeked over her shoulder, but quickly whipped her head back because Charlot had been watching. If her heart pounded any faster, it might jump from her chest and race across the lake like Grandpa's skiff.

"I need to wait for the fire to burn down so I can use the ash to wash everything." Her tone matched the despondency in her heart, and she silently cursed her damned vulnerability.

"Not a problem. It shall die soon." He stood. "While we are waiting, why not show me how to use your weapon?"

She made her way back to him, plates shaking thanks to her dumb hands turning traitor. "I can do that. I also need to bathe. I can use the ashes, can I not?" She thrust her chin at the fire.

He chuckled. "Of course. How do you think your sister washed up while she was here? Come." He grabbed his musket.

Alma set down the plates and grabbed her rifle before following him.

"It repeats, hmm." He nodded at her weapon.

"Yes. I will show you how I load it."

Theodore trotted beside them.

"And I shall do the same." He stopped at an old fallen tree. "You trained him well. He is a good dog."

"Thank you." When Charlot thought to pat Theodore on the head, warmth flooded her chest.

She surveyed the area. Charlot had chosen a perfect spot because there was another half-broken, dead tree they could use as a target.

He held the musket parallel to the ground. "You must start at this angle."

Alma eased the big gun from him. It was heavier than her rifle—much heavier. But she had strong biceps from all of her tomboy activities.

Charlot reached for something on his hip. A paper cartridge, which he handed to her. "This contains your powder and ball. Half cock the hammer and open the pan first. Right here."

She opened the pan.

"Tear open the top of the cartridge and pour some powder into the pan."

Only some? Why not all of it? But she held her tongue, or she'd annoy him, and they might start bickering again. Nothing was going to cost her this experience of firing an ancient weapon.

"Set the butt of the musket on the ground."

Again, she followed his orders.

"Pour the rest down the barrel, followed by the paper containing the ball."

She emptied the last of the powder and then stuffed the paper-wrapped ball down the barrel.

"This is the ramrod." He pointed. "Release it and pack the powder."

This was too exciting and interesting. She did as ordered.

"Three times or more to ensure it's packed tight."

She performed the packing until he gave a brisk nod.

"Recover the ramrod."

She secured the long, wooden stick in its spot beneath the barrel.

"Finally, fully cock the hammer." He pointed at it again.

She knew where the hammer was but didn't tell him she didn't need that much instruction, or they'd be ready to choke one another for the eighteenth time.

"You are now ready to fire. Turn to your target."

Excitement fluttered through her veins. "How long of a shot do you get with this?" She aimed at the broken tree.

"Watch and see."

She was about three hundred yards from her target.

"Use the front post sight and the rear notch. Line them up with the spot on the tree you wish to hit."

"I have it in my sight." More excitement fluttered inside of her.

"Fire when ready."

Her finger itched, ready to fire, but she made sure she had everything properly lined up. Hitting her target was imperative. She squeezed. The boom echoed through the trees. The recoil wasn't as bad as she'd assumed, nothing close to the kick from her rifle.

"Ah, *magnifique*." He brought his hands together in a low, lazy clap.

The rush sent the blood racing to her head. So much so that she was ready to squeal like a pig running about in an enclosure. A true adrenaline rush. "That was... Goodness. I enjoyed that very much." If only she could use English to say *fuck yeah, baby*!

"May I try again?"

"We must be careful with ammunition, unfortunately."

"I understand." She licked her lips. God, she couldn't get over the heady pleasure she received from target shooting with him by her side.

"Now it is my turn." He raised one brow, smirking at the rifle she'd set on the ground.

"You will enjoy this very much," she reassured him, matching his smirk.

"Oh? Will I? By the look in your eyes, you seem to find weapons more pleasurable than..." He kept grinning, and his twinkling gaze said he more than implied a sexual innuendo.

"I would not know what lying with a man means because I never engaged." She didn't know where the bold words came from, but she couldn't help lifting her stare to meet his, still smirking.

"I expected as much. You are young. A maiden." His smile was teasing, tickling her insides. "I guess you will first have to engage in coupling before you can decide which is better."

"I guess I will have to." She couldn't believe she'd said that, much less was having such a conversation.

The silent pause reminded her she was alone, in the past, with a stranger.

"You did not ask if you would have someone to teach you coupling." He continued to grin.

"That's because I am busy teaching someone how to use this." She reached for her rifle before the conversation became too seductive for her ears.

He snickered. "Very well."

She almost couldn't believe he'd finally acknowledged she was of the opposite sex. Not that he hadn't before. What counted was that perhaps he had truly taken a good, long look and had found something interesting.

She offered up her weapon, which she'd made sure to empty first. "Like you taught me, I'll show you how to load it. First, we turn on what is called the safety."

"Safety?"

"Yes, it makes sure that you cannot fire it."

"Hmm..." He nodded and moved his finger to where she pointed and engaged the safety.

"This is the action. It is where we will load the bullets."

"No ball? Powder?"

She shook her head, handing him the first bullet. "Open it by pulling the bolt handle up and back toward you."

He did as she told him.

"We are going to load the bullets to fill what is called the"—she wasn't sure how to translate the word *magazine* in Ojibway—"container. Set the pointed end in first, then press down until you hear a click."

"Interesting." He loaded the ten bullets she'd set into his palm.

"Now close the bolt just the opposite of how you had opened it."

The clicking of the cartridge fed and locked into the chamber broke into the stillness of the forest, telling her he'd done the loading correctly. Of course he was a natural. He said he'd been firing guns his whole life. "You are ready."

"Ah...there are two sights just like my musket." He had one eye closed while sighting the rifle.

She wasn't surprised she didn't have to tell him that. "Yes."

Before she could offer more instructions, he squeezed the trigger.

He automatically operated the side bolt to eject the spent casing and racked another into place. Again, without needing any instructions, he fired another shot.

Both hit their targets—dead center of the tree.

"My apologies." He even remembered to engage the safety. "But I could not resist since you told me this repeats. And it does." Delight shone in his eyes. "Such a marvelous weapon. *Magnifique*. If not for the importance of preserving our ammunition, I would enjoy firing again."

He made sure and aimed the end of the rifle at the ground, even with the safety on, as he picked up the two casings. "One cannot leave this out here. It is an insult to the beauty of this land, and a sign of your presence."

"Yes, it is." Something Grandpa had told her whenever they hunted.

"I must admit, I truly like this weapon." He held the rifle parallel, his gaze moving up and down the barrel, as if sliding his gaze over the shape of a woman's hips and breasts.

Heat crawled along Alma's face. Boy, there was a lot of that going on as of late.

"Tell me, is this the weapon of this supposed future then?"

She nodded. "It is, but I must say I really admire your musket. Even if it is heavy."

"Yes. Heavy indeed. But yours is very light." He held the rifle with one hand, still checking out the details.

"It is. They are much lighter."

"I believe you would be more comfortable using this?" He handed over the rifle.

"Of course. Grandpa made sure when he bought me the gun, he gave me one suitable for my weight." She took her rifle, which she reloaded.

"I wish we could continue partaking in this marvelous activity, but alas, we must preserve our ammunition." He also reloaded his.

"Yes, we should." The longer they stared, the more she got the sinking feeling of spinach between her teeth. Maybe only on her part. She couldn't believe Charlot had ever known an awkward moment in his life.

"Then we shall return..." He gestured with his hand, motioning for her to go first like a gentleman in a historical movie.

But she had no desire to return to the lake. Standing in the middle of a forest with him, both holding their guns, his face reflecting his excitement over firing her rifle, she couldn't help but feel the seduction written all over his high cheekbones, green eyes, and pink mouth.

"*Mademoiselle?*" he teased. "Ladies first."

"Yes. First." She wet her lips. This was a moment when she wished she could speak in English. Maybe that was why he sometimes reverted to French instead of *Anishinaabemowin*. He probably found words in his natural language easier to convey his true emotional thoughts.

She started down the path they'd cut to reach their camp. His footsteps followed behind her, and Theodore trotted by her side. "You should probably rest."

"Yes, my pipe and then a quick sleep will suffice."

She glanced behind her. He was using his stick to walk.

"Did you want me to carry your musket?" The weapon was heavy, and he probably wished to hold his side.

"I am fine. We only have a short walk."

After a bit more stepping through the woods, they reached the lake where they had claimed their camping spot. She wasn't sure how she'd pass the time while he napped.

He sat on his bedroll, laying the musket beside him, and removed his ammunition pouch before lying back.

Maybe she'd swim. The coals had burned down. She could make a concoction from the ashes to wash the grime from her skin.

Charlot rested his hands on his flat stomach, tangling his fingers. He seemed to forget about smoking his pipe.

Alma gathered up the ashes and headed for the water. Once she had fashioned a good enough scrub to wash with, she shed her clothing, ensuring to stay behind the bushes for privacy in case Charlot woke.

Stripping naked produced goosebumps over her skin, and not from the cold because the hot sun of summer beat down on her.

She drew in a big breath and moved off the rock and into the water. This was the first time her naked body had experienced the lake since she always wore a swimsuit or swimming shorts. But being without clothes was wickedly delightful and even exhilarating.

Theodore jumped in after her. He began swimming about.

"Does it feel good?" she asked her dog while wading in deeper.

"Did you need me to make you something for bathing?"

The question caused Alma to freeze.

Charlot!

Any second, he'd appear around the bush.

She ducked beneath the water, only allowing her head to be seen just as Charlot rounded the bend.

Chapter Ten: Stuck on You

CHARLOT HADN'T EXPECTED to find Arms Oneself with her clothes off. *Mon Dieu*! No wonder she sank beneath the water, only her lovely face—the color of a tomato—visible.

A gentleman would cover his eyes. Time ticked away before he finally forced his lustful gaze to agree with his brain, and he squeezed his eyes shut. Only a silly man turned away from a beautiful maiden in the lake without her clothes on. "I see you have no need for some ash."

"I..." She cleared her throat. There was a splash.

He cracked open his lids slightly. "You have made some?"

"Y-yes."

Her stammering was as lyrical as her native tongue.

"Very well. Enjoy your bathing." He had to force himself to turn around, even when his body hollered at him to take advantage of the stunning lass by peeling off his own clothes and joining her in the water.

He forced himself to walk. As he moved along, the walking branch tapped against the rocks, creating distance between them that he did not wish for. He muttered under his breath, "*Tu sot.*"

Goodness, how was he supposed to sleep when Arms Oneself was without clothing? Her breasts weren't very big, but he could imagine how stunning those bronze globes would appear with water streaming over them, even coaxing her nipples to a full erection. Sweet nipples, probably tastier than the berries the brother of summer blessed on the land. What about the hair between her legs? He could almost smell the aroma her womanly region gave off. Imagine her washing such a personal area. Her fingers gliding between her womanly lips, stripping her sheath of its natural flavor. A perfume he enjoyed sniffing while lying with a lovely *mademoiselle*.

It had been a long time since he'd last enjoyed bedding down with a woman. Most maidens were kept close to their families. But whenever he arrived at one of the villages or camps, one somehow slithered away from prying eyes to steal off with him. So far, he'd been lucky not to be challenged by a brother or father, probably because he always brought gifts to the Indians, something

63

they enjoyed. And he'd be considered rude not to appear with gifts, since the *Saulteurs* expected as much.

He sat back on his bedroll, gaze wandering to the bush where Arms Oneself shielded herself from him. Was she washing her slim yet firm arms with a nice, lovely rounding of muscles? Such strength she possessed, but lean.

He glanced down at his breeches, his staff standing at attention, but he couldn't help his arousal. Again, he peered toward the bush. A gentleman would stay put. But he didn't wish to play the gentleman.

ALMA FINISHED WASHING. Even though she liked to swim after cleaning up, that wouldn't happen this time. Not with Charlot mere steps away.

The look in his eyes, the way he'd caressed her flesh beneath the water when he'd stood on the bank still left her shivering, even breathless. To further irritate her—or would it be arouse?—she kept sneaking looks his way, her heart holding its beat, hoping he'd appear from behind the thick bush where she hid.

A warrior never bothered a maiden, according to Edie, but Charlot was French. He had his own set of beliefs. Edie had even called him a rogue. Alma giggled at the word. In the twenty-first century, they'd use the term *player*.

She adored his roguish ways, though. The naughty glint in his piercing green eyes, the half-smile only a wolf could emulate before pouncing on a helpless rabbit. They were both hunters, both experienced with guns, both outdoors people.

She ran her tongue along her lower lip. This was stupid. Pathetic. Hiding in the water, hoping he'd appear. Maybe he'd fallen asleep. The longer she remained, the disappointment in her belly said he wasn't coming.

Shoulders heavy, she forced herself to walk toward the shoreline. The more she inched her way to the big, flat rock, the more she exposed her flesh, which the sun's warm rays kissed.

Part of her kept hoping to get caught, the other part, made up of pure modesty and self-deprecation, feared Charlot would find her exposed, and worse, wrinkle his nose and run off into the woods.

She reached the shore with no sign of him. Sniffing the air didn't produce the scent of tobacco, so he must have fallen asleep as he said he would. With no

She gasped.

He disappeared beneath the surface.

She couldn't help herself and skulked around the bush.

He resurfaced, his shoulder-length hair pushed off his face, allowing a wonderful view of his long forehead and straight nose. Beads of water snaked down his cheekbones. He swam out further, and his back muscles flexed with his movement.

At least his butt was under the water, or she would've overheated. Yes, spying was wrong. Very wrong. She would've been horrified if he'd stolen a peek at her from behind the bush.

Or would she have?

No.

She bowed her head.

Dammit. English thoughts came fast, easier to capture than the Ojibway language, which had invaded her tongue from the moment she stepped from the dancing flames.

Charlot ceased to swim.

She quickly ducked behind the bush again.

He treaded water for a moment, staring at the bush.

Oh geez, had he spied her?

He proceeded to swim again, this time on his back, stroking his arms through the water, giving her a—heaven help her—long look at his flat stomach and...

Oh boy.

The *and* was ten times worse.

Or should that be ten times better?

It was right there for her to look at.

His cock.

Limp.

Yet, with one touch, his flaccid flesh could become powerful and erect.

She squeezes her eyes shut.

Go back to the campfire.

But she couldn't.

Something had glued her feet to the rock she balanced on. Hunger surfaced, an overpowering need to leave the bush, shed her clothes, and join him in the water.

How bold.

Edie never would've put herself in this kind of position.

But she wasn't Edie. She was Alma. Alma, who'd been in trouble from day one for being too independent, too obstinate, and too much like her father.

Charlot kept swimming on his back toward the shore.

She licked her lips, unable to tear her gaze from the flaccid flesh resting between his lean-muscled thighs.

Heat grew between her legs. Insurmountable heat, needing something. Anything.

He rolled off his back and stood. Reaching beneath the surface, he grabbed up a handful of sand that he ran along his arms.

Alma wet her lips as he massaged the tiny grains along his smooth tanned flesh. He kept teasing her with the slow strokes he bestowed on his skin. Once he finished, he glided his palms along his legs.

She couldn't help shifting to all fours to crawl in closer.

The more he caressed himself, the fiercer the heat grew, until she swore a fire raged inside of her.

He turned then, gazing at the shoreline.

Alma kept close to the rock.

"*Ma chérie*," he called out. "How much longer are you going to hide there? The water is perfect. If you wish to swim again, instead of lurking about, come in. I will not mind."

She slapped her hand over her mouth.

The bastard.

All along, he knew she'd been watching him.

His swimming, his cleansing his skin... It'd all been a show for her.

She wasn't sure if she should cuss him out or...blush.

Cussing won.

She stood.

He kept grinning.

Chapter Eleven: Hard for Love

"WELL?" HIS QUESTION was coated with the same teasing strokes he'd lavished with sand on his arms moments before.

Alma stomped closer until she stood on the rock leading into the water. "I have already swum."

"Then why lurk about?" He rinsed the sand from his arms as he pushed his marvelous body against the water, inching in closer.

Alma stiffened. There was no way she'd run like a coward, as he probably expected her to do. She'd wanted to see him naked, and he'd damned well had obliged. "Maybe I am not lurking?"

"Are you not?" He motioned at the bush, his smile on the sardonic side. "Then what would you call this?"

The dryness in her throat didn't allow for a rebuttal.

"Would you have been offended if I had spied on you?" He kept coming closer, the light treasure trail of hair growing bolder, exposing his lower stomach, almost sitting where...

Alma drew back her shoulders. "Not at all. As a matter of fact, I kept looking for you, but you never came."

"Ah, you suspected me of not behaving as a gentleman should? Even out here, I am a gentleman. It is how I was raised."

She nodded.

"Or did you hope I'd behave as a rogue?" His grin turned sly.

She gasped. How had he guessed her thoughts?

"Aha, so you did. Hmm?" He was close enough to allow her gaze to follow exactly where his treasure trail led.

With his cock floating on the water's surface, she had a clear view of his swelling girth.

Swelling for her.

She placed her hand on her chest to calm her heart. If she didn't settle her breathing, her lungs would burst from her chest.

"Then join me if you wish..." He angled his head to the side.

Join him? In the water? Naked? Her?

Knees quivering, she threw out her arms to steady herself before she fell face-first in the water. Not the impression she wanted to give to her dream man...

Who was here.

And very much real.

Offering her a chance to swim in the lake with him...naked.

"Did you need any help?" The way his brow popped slightly indicated he'd meant her clothes.

She touched the hem of her shirt. All she had to do was slip it over her head. Then remove her tank top. The boots would be a bitch to toss off before she could wriggle out of her camouflage pants, requiring her to sit on the rock.

Well, she could do that.

It was a start. Right?

She carefully sat on the slightly sloping rock.

His eyes crinkled. He was probably wondering what she was doing.

She leaned over and unlaced one of her boots.

The curiosity in his eyes vanished, and his gaze became intense and smoky deep.

She'd never seen him look *that* way before. Was this how he appeared when aroused?

As she unlaced the other boot, her breathing quickened. All she had to do was tug them off. With shaking hands, she freed her feet.

Next, she worked on her socks.

He kept watching.

Being the object of his seductive stare made removing the items nearly impossible.

The look he cast seemed to grip her by the shoulders, forcing her to keep eye contact, boldly demanding she not break the stare.

Once she tossed aside her socks, she inched down the rock but stopped where the water lapped at her toes. Uncertainty crashed against her like a giant wave. She was about to strip naked. In front of Charlot. The man who'd haunted her dreams.

Mom was right. Alma never thought about the consequences of her actions, assuming everything would work out perfectly.

Charlot's palms skimmed through the water, still staring.

With a big breath of self-encouragement, Alma unsnapped the button on her camouflage pants.

"Interesting. I never complimented you on how well what you wear blends in with the environment. I have seen your people do this many times when engaging in warfare."

She wasn't about to tell him it was standard in the twenty-first century.

She took a deep breath and lowered the zipper. The *zrup* was loud enough to wake the dead. Her knees kept quivering as Charlot continued to stare while running his hands through the water.

She lowered the pants, exposing her underwear.

Curiosity pierced his gaze since he darn well hadn't seen a woman in panties before, and lord knew when those had been invented. He'd probably expected a slip of some sort to be beneath her clothes.

"*Chérie*," he murmured with delight.

She quickly removed her shirt, followed by her tank top, before she lost her nerve.

He set his finger on his mouth, shaking his head. "I have never seen such..." The awe in his voice said he more than enjoyed her underwear, even if it was a plain white bra and cotton panties.

All that was left to shed was her final layer of protection. Her heart moved to her throat, almost choking her.

Charlot ran his tongue along his lower lip, as if wanting a taste of the bare skin she had exposed.

Shivering, she reached behind and unsnapped the bra.

His eyes widened, wiping away the sly look he'd previously offered.

With her hands still shaking, she slid the straps from her shoulders, slowly baring her breasts before dropping the bra to the ground. The rays from the sun hit her skin, but goosebumps peppered her flesh. Although modesty screamed *cover yourself*, she pushed away the nagging and hooked her thumbs into her bikini briefs.

Even though her feet longed to run back behind the bush, Alma forced the panties down inch by inch, almost cringing.

Charlot moved in closer, his admiring gaze fixed between her legs. "*Ma chérie*, come here."

She dropped the panties, quaking.

"There is nothing to be afraid of," he reassured her.

She dipped one foot into the lake. This helped cool her rapidly heating skin.

Charlot stepped forward, coming closer, the water giving way to his firm body.

Alma submerged her other foot, drawing in a big breath. She could take this one moment with her and hug the memories close once she returned to the twenty-first century.

The water only reached Charlot's thighs. His cock stood proud, a true indication of his desire. But according to Edie, Charlot desired every maiden. He was a man determined to live by his own rules, spend his life in the interior until he grew too old. Then, just like his father, he would return to Montréal when age got the better of him.

A loner.

A man meant to walk without a companion.

He drew his arms around her waist.

His touch sent pure electrical excitement buzzing between Alma's legs. He was close enough to smell. Even taste. The water continued to trickle from his hair along the lean planes of his face, dipping into the hollows of his cheeks. A droplet clung to his prominent chin.

Gosh, he was gorgeous. Too damned handsome.

"Are you ready for this?" His soft words caressed her skin. "You can always turn back."

Turn back?

Was he crazy?

She'd dreamt about this moment.

"I am ready."

"You are shivering."

She couldn't blame the cold because she'd arrived here in the middle of July. Fine, she'd own the truth, and if he behaved like an ass, spoiling this wonderful moment, she'd drown him. "I am nervous."

"There is nothing to be nervous about. What we are about to do is perfectly natural. What we enjoy out here is as natural as the turning of the seasons. As natural as nature itself." He lifted his hand to indicate the forest. The water in his palm drained from between his open fingers.

His reassuring words touched a spot she didn't think existed. He could be a true gentleman. "I know it is natural." She wet her lips.

His gaze followed the movement of her tongue.

Part of her yearned to squirm, even back away, but the bold girl hiding in her ached for this too bad. Edie was now a wife and mother, even though her older sister was only twenty. But in this century, they'd be considered fully mature women ready for a home, husband, and family.

Charlot leaned forward, closing his eyes.

Before she could think or digest what was happening, his mouth came down over hers. His sensual attack unleashed a storm within her. One filled with lightning and crackling heat. She never experienced such tenderness from lips before, marked with desire as his mouth tasted hers.

This wasn't anything like the kiss she'd received at a dance. Nor was Charlot a boy. He was a man in the raw, who had dared to draw her into the deepest temptation of her life. And it was easy to return what Charlot offered. So what if she ignored the consequences of her actions?

Charlot had shifted from a nightmare into the sweetest dream possible.

He drew her closer, molding her breasts against his chest covered in hair, just enough to sprinkle him with pure manliness. Being so close to pure masculinity left her lightheaded, and she returned the kiss. The heat on her skin became a fire. Almost torturous with the curiosity of where their dance would lead.

He glided his calloused fingers along her spine, tracing the tiny bumps. Shivers exploded through her, the good kind that toyed with what lay hidden between her legs. His hard cock pressing on her belly produced more chills. The excitement bubbling between her legs became out of control. She had no choice but to accept his silken kisses that were growing hungrier, close to tasting her.

He ran his tongue along her mouth.

She almost gasped, having never experienced that kind of move before. Charlot's searching kiss left her eager, wanting more. Without having to think about her next move, her arms naturally wrapped his neck. She wiggled in closer until his cock was pressed tight between them. Her body had taken over, and she loved how it guided her in what Charlot had called natural.

His tongue slid into her mouth and toyed with hers, and she joined him in the dance, a seductive one that created more heat. She gripped him firmer around the neck, tilting her head to the side to create a perfect fit. The tobacco he loved to smoke danced on her taste buds.

Maybe this was where she belonged—with Charlot in the past. She'd searched forever for the spot where she fit, and the eighteenth century seemed the perfect place, a place where her sister had also found true peace.

Charlot was made for the woods. And so was she.

He needed a companion who could keep up with him, a self-sufficient partner capable of living in the wilderness.

His fingers kept dancing up and down her spine, teasing her skin until her hips wiggled, and she rubbed up against him, tasting his flesh with her own.

His tongue continued to explore hers. He traced his fingers from the middle of her back to the spot where her spine ended. Her breathing jumped, aware of the place he sought. And he did, tracing a path to the cleft of her buttocks. The excitement unfurling between her legs became a hothouse of coals.

She wanted this.

Wanted it bad.

She wanted him to touch her *there*.

His fingers moved lower until they grazed her cheeks.

The pleasure hidden beneath her pussy lips became smoother than silk. Slippery. Wet and erotic.

Theodore yipped.

Charlot broke the kiss.

Alma's heart almost came to a full stop. Charlot might as well have dumped a bucket of ice over her head. Had she done something wrong? Disappointment weighed as heavy as a load of lead in her stomach.

"I heard something." He released her, glancing around.

"Heard something?" Her mind remained on their kiss, and she had to shake her head, attempting to follow his lead by searching their surroundings.

"I thought I heard someone approaching. Quick. To the shore."

What if the intruder was the Dakota?

"My rifle..." Dammit, she should have heeded Theodore's warning.

"Come..." Charlot grabbed her hand, steering her to the big rock where she'd left her clothes. "We must scout the area."

He led them quickly through the water while pressing his free hand over his wound.

Alma's stomach seemed to fall to her ankles. Moving quickly was difficult for him. "We need to find you a hiding spot while I search the area."

"Hiding spot?" He blanched just as they reached the rock. "I will not hide. I will go with you."

"But you're in no shape to—"

"Do not tell me what I can or cannot do," he snapped, almost crushing her fingers. "I said I will help you, and I will."

Oh great, after a perfect moment in the water, he was back to his usual pissy self.

Wait, she had no place to complain. Something was out there, something Theodore and Charlot had heard, but she'd failed to notice.

Some damned warrior she'd turned out to be, having failed all because of her stupid clit.

Chapter Twelve: Warriors

CHARLOT SNATCHED UP his clothing, having no time to dry off. If the Sioux were present, they could be seeking revenge. He had a young woman to take into consideration, even if she professed to be a warrior. A woman was a woman, no matter what she claimed to be.

Beside him, Arms Oneself didn't dry off either. She wiggled into the strange wear she wore beneath her outer garments. Once dressed, she seized her weapon.

Charlot didn't bother reaching for the branch he used as a cane. He needed to carry his musket since it'd be too heavy for Arms Oneself, although her rifle could fire many rounds at a time. He grabbed her by the hand and led her to safety.

Just as he reached the campfire where he'd left his musket, an arrow tore by him, the tip piercing a nearby tree. He didn't look over his shoulder but snatched up his weapon. He whirled on his heel, staying behind a rock.

Arms Oneself ducked behind him, checking her rifle.

The dog never barked or growled, but its flat ears and bared teeth said it was ready to attack if given the command. At least they didn't have to worry about the animal's interference.

"Stay down," he ordered, attempting to sight the movement in the bushes.

"I can fire one shot after another," Arms Oneself reminded him. "Cover me."

He stifled his grunt, although a man's job was to protect women. A wave of *déjà vu* hit him, having done this already with Fire Woman.

He used the muzzle of the musket to trace the forest, but nothing came into view. He closed his eyes, straining to listen for even a leaf to fall, but no sound came.

"What do you think it is?" she whispered.

"I do not know." He kept his voice low, still scouting the area. "It fired at me. Look at the tree."

She covered her mouth.

"They are patient. Very patient. They are waiting for us to let down our guard. Be vigilant."

"Do you think they will surround us?" She glanced toward her dog, who continued to stare at her, ears perked.

"They cannot, unless they cross the lake. It is why I prefer these types of locations. I can see everything coming at me and keep my back to the water."

"Is it the Sioux?"

"I will not know until I look at the arrow. Your kind has unique ways of constructing them. Because of the attack on your sister's village, it could be your people."

Arms Oneself shivered.

"Do not shiver now, brave one. Show me the courage you came with when you first arrived. Remember, we are in a true animal environment out here. You either let nature take its course, or you retaliate. We must retaliate."

She nodded, face tight.

He returned to scanning the woods, but nothing appeared. "We cannot take a chance if they are firing at us."

She readied her rifle.

His peripheral vision caught the flicker of a feather. "There," he hissed.

She pointed the end of her gun at the target he'd identified and fired.

A shout came from behind the tree.

"He is hit." Charlot kept scoping the area, attempting to locate another foe.

He spotted two. One darted through the trees, the opening in the branches offering a glimpse of the warrior's feathers, while the other slithered behind a rock.

"Get the one running," he ordered her.

Charlot readied his musket and scooted onto his belly. He crawled across the ground, each push forward creating a fire in his wounded side. He clenched his teeth. Now was not the time to acknowledge the pain. The one warrior had hidden himself, probably burrowing in deep somewhere.

The Sioux did not have muskets, only the *Saulteurs,* since his fellow fur traders did business with them. Nor did he feel sorry for the Sioux for being driven out by Arms Oneself's people. Over time, with how the interior was slowly being infiltrated by forts, the *Saulteurs* would find themselves in the same predicament.

To hide his presence, he kept creeping along the forest floor, a slow process to ensure he didn't snap any twigs or crumple leaves. Maybe the Sioux had thought he'd fled with Arms Oneself, pursuing the warrior's comrade.

A gunshot exploded through the air, far from where he crawled. If the Sioux only had bows and arrows, this meant Arms Oneself had hopefully found her target.

He continued to worm his way along the forest floor, relieved she was safe. However, he shouldn't have worried. She'd told him too many times she could take care of herself, which she was more than proving.

Footprints.

Aha.

He was closing in on his foe. The Sioux had buried himself deep somewhere, hidden by the foliage and rocks. A mosquito buzzed around Charlot's head. A sharp sting sprang up on the back of his neck, but he did not dare slap the pesky bug. Being poked went with living inside the interior. There'd be time to scratch the bite later. Right now, he had to keep his focus.

He continued to follow the tracks that took him beneath a few low spruce boughs. Then he slithered around a few rocks. He stifled his grunt, doing his best to ignore the pain digging into his side.

Somehow, he must calm his breathing, or the warrior would hear him, but crawling with a musket and an injury proved to be a trying task.

An arrow whirled by his head.

He flinched.

A feather appeared in his line of vision. The warrior had to reload. This gave Charlot the chance to stand tall. He aimed his musket, finger on the trigger, and squeezed just as the warrior, also standing, drew back his bow. Once Charlot fired, he dropped to the ground. Nothing but a thud infiltrated the forest.

It might be a trick.

Charlot stayed on the ground while attempting to reload the musket.

The warrior screamed. He jumped from the bush with a raised tomahawk, blood spewing from his chest.

With no time to reload, Charlot grabbed the end of the musket and swung it at the warrior.

As the warrior readied to strike, a blast pierced Charlot's ears. But the Sioux tumbled to the forest floor, eyes open, and his wounded chest completely soaked with blood.

Charlot whipped around.

Arms Oneself stood by a tree away from him, still holding her rifle with the dog beside her.

He did not know if he should thank her or whoop her bottom.

ALMA LOWERED HER RIFLE, her teeth clattering and knees shaking. The weight of her body almost took her to the ground. If she moved, she'd fall over.

She was not meant to be here. Mother was right—she acted and never thought about the consequences.

"What are you doing?" Charlot stormed toward her.

At that moment, she wasn't in the mood to deal with his pissy temperament, not after taking a life. Bile rose in her throat, and her teeth kept chattering. But she'd had no choice. It'd come down to the warrior's or Charlot's lives, and she'd chosen the ungrateful jerk.

They hadn't sought out the warrior to kill him. The warrior had hunted them, and in turn she'd defended the man who'd stolen her heart. An undeserving man whose narrowed eyes and straight mouth said he wanted to read her the riot act.

"Don't you dare," she growled. "Not after I saved your sorry ass."

His mouth fell open. The confusion in his eyes said he hadn't understood a word she'd spoken.

She almost smacked herself because she'd spoken in English, a language he could not comprehend, and she sure as shit didn't speak French.

"Do not lecture me." She held up her hand. "I was defending you. You would have done the same for me. We are partners out here, are we not?"

"*Oui.*" He nodded, but annoyance still glimmered in his eyes.

"I have killed someone for the first time." A lump grew in her throat. "I am in no mood for arguments or..."

She whipped on her heel and fled, not caring if there could be more Sioux in the area, not caring she might startle a bear feasting on blueberries, not caring what lay ahead as she pushed through the thick underbrush with Theodore on her heels. Twigs whipped at her face, stinging her cheeks.

"Enough." Charlot's words came hot on her neck.

Alma didn't stop to wait for him. She kept running for the campsite. All she needed to do was grab her backpack and get the fuck out of here, leave before something else happened that she'd regret.

She almost tripped over a rock in the path but steadied herself. Just as she reached the camp, Charlot's strong fingers encircled her wrist.

"Control yourself," he ordered. "Look at me."

She clenched her jaw.

"I said look at me, Arms Oneself."

She turned her head to meet his fiery gaze.

"You knew of the dangers when you came here. You knew there would be a battle. You armed yourself, prepared to fight the Sioux to save me. And that was what you did only moments ago."

When she attempted to cast her anger at the tree, his fingers gripped her face so she couldn't look away.

"*Ma chérie*, understand this. Killing is part of warfare."

"I did not wish to engage in a war." She bit back the lump that grew bigger in her throat.

"But you have. And this will not be your last time if you are to remain out here. Do you think warriors take pride in killing?"

"They must, because they dance around with the scalps of their foes, regaling everyone in song about their feats."

"Yes, it is a time to celebrate. But they are celebrating another day above ground. Not celebrating the people they must kill. Their fight is about life. Do you know what survival is where you come from? Because survival is difficult for all. Even the birds. The insects. Everything that exists is fighting to live.

"The flowers crowd out other flowers, determined to take in the most sunlight. The same for the trees. Even the vegetation is intent on killing to survive.

"Your sister told me the animals are the teachers of the *Saulteurs*. She is correct. Just as they must kill to live, so do you. They do not murder for the sake of murdering. Or for jewels. Or pretty baubles. Greedily taking what they wish.

"Even your dog..." He pointed at Theodore. "Your dog will kill for you if you so much as give the order. And once he kills, he will not feel guilty for protecting his pack. Nothing more.

"You have done what must be done. Take the warrior's scalp. Celebrate. For you have a right to. A defeat of the enemy means another day above ground, and another day above ground for me, for you did what a warrior does—kills for the people."

Alma brought her fingers to her lower lip. He was right. She had come armed and ready for battle to save him from the fate he'd faced when Edie had gone back through the dancing flames.

Before she could think, she threw her arms around him. His scent invaded her nostrils. She held tight to his lean muscles that flexed beneath her palms. "*Meegwetch*."

"You do not need to thank me. I am simply reminding you of who you truly are, what your people have taught you to be."

"I came here so you could continue to live, and it is what I have done," she murmured.

"Then we shall celebrate with food and dance, just like your people do. What of the other warrior?"

"He managed to get away. I hit his buttock. We must move our camp. Once he returns to his people, he will tell them what happened."

"There are many lakes out here. I shall go east toward another. I can leave right away."

She lay her head on his shoulder. "Do you not mean *we*?"

"It will take us further from where the dancing flames are. Is that not where you wish to go? I am healing. I do believe I can carry on."

She lifted her head from his shoulder, staring into his eyes that told her nothing of whether he regretted her leaving.

But she wasn't ready to leave, even after taking a life, which continued to gnaw at her conscience.

"I will go with you. You are not healed enough."

He touched her face, his soft fingers caressing her flesh. "*Ma chérie*, is this an excuse to remain with me?"

Alma swallowed. He was more than capable of finding the other lake he spoke about.

"I..." She blinked. "I..."

"Not ready to leave?"

She'd always searched for where she belonged. The only place she'd felt comfortable was with Grandpa, out on the lake canoeing, or fishing, or trekking through the forest hunting.

"Come, then." He motioned at their belongings. "We will go. You can regale me with your tale during your dance tonight."

Chapter Thirteen: Gutter Ballet

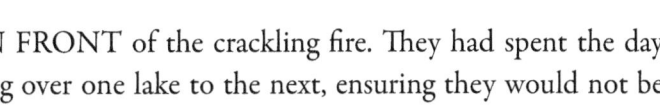

CHARLOT SAT IN FRONT of the crackling fire. They had spent the day traveling, even passing over one lake to the next, ensuring they would not be faced with another Sioux attack. One more portage and they could be on the big lake, paddling for *Lac à la Pluie*, where the fort was located, standing tall on the point.

For the moment, he'd enjoy the dance performed by Arms Oneself, a woman he did not wish to see leave when they'd spoken of her inevitable departure earlier. He'd brought up the subject, if he was honest, to test her. See if she truly wanted to find the dancing flames to return to this strange place in the future where she professed to be from.

His musket rested beside him, loaded and ready to fire, in case the stealthy Sioux did track them. But he doubted any warriors would make an appearance this night. The one man who'd managed to get away might have bled out before reaching help. But he could have also lived, for the Sioux were a sly bunch, hence their name of little snakes. The warrior could've easily found a way to doctor himself, something Charlot's father had taught him to survive, since it was the Indians who'd shown his kind how to outwit death.

Arms Oneself had professed to knowing only one song, which was the dance for hunters capturing an animal.

How strange she failed to know such an important song, for he'd witnessed warriors dancing many times, recounting their tales of defeating their enemies. She'd also refused the scalp he'd claimed for her. It sat on a pole, drying out. He'd never known a warrior to pass up a scalp. Perhaps females did not take them.

Arms Oneself's dancing wasn't seductive, but that of a butterfly breaking free from the cocoon, soaring and fluttering about a flower. She twirled, using the blanket like a shawl, while she sprang and hopped about the fire, always keeping one arm horizontal. Even her singing overpowered the starlit night. A song of freedom and power.

As for the dog, the big beast sat beside him, watching his mistress.

Arms Oneself stopped, glancing over her shoulder to gaze at him.

He clapped. "That was very beautiful."

"*Meegwetch*." She bowed her head. "I had to improvise."

"You did?" He reached for his pipe.

"Yes. Where I come from, I am a fancy shawl dancer. My sister is a jingle dress dancer."

"I have not heard of either."

"You would not have, for they have not been invented yet."

She seemed to revel in reminding him about this future place.

"Our regalia is even different. Mine is..." She licked her lips. "Let us say we took full advantage of the pretty ribbons and material you have at your forts. I am a butterfly."

"What about those steps? They reminded me of a crow on the ground."

"That is the crow hop. We also do that when we dance. Crow is a very important bird. He helps us find our purpose. An aid to others."

"Did he help you find your purpose while you danced?"

She glanced away.

He had to ask, although it was none of his business, but something coaxed him to inquire. "Tell me, are you happy from whence you came?"

Her jawline stiffened.

"Or are you still seeking your purpose?"

"Maybe I am," she whispered, still staring into the distance.

"You are a warrior, though."

She nodded. "I am that. But for who and what?" Her eyes crinkled.

"Perhaps you are meant to be here...why you came here?"

Her dark eyes glittered. "But I came here to help, not to find myself."

"Maybe that is what this is all about. I know Fire Woman was very happy and had no desire to leave. I had to push her into the dancing flames."

"She told me so. She said you used your foot and gave her backside a good shove."

They both chuckled.

"Come. Sit with me." He patted the spot beside him.

She remained wrapped in the blanket and sank down beside him.

Although the night was warm, he liked the blanket on her, reminding him of how the women among the *Saulteurs* dressed.

"You dance very well. You will have to learn the warrior's dance."

"Maybe..."

He yearned to nuzzle her neck, even kiss the soft skin. Something unsettling cramped his stomach. Would she allow him? Why was he hesitating? He'd known how to seduce women since he first left home with his father and had entered the interior. What was it about this young woman who left him on the defensive, scratching his head?

WHEN THE DAKOTA HAD interrupted the intimate moment with Charlot at the lake earlier in the day, Alma didn't think there'd be another opportunity. But they were far from the dancing flames where the Dakota now resided. They might even stay there. The land where the Ojibway summer camp was located could've been the reason why the Dakota had attacked her people.

"Do you think the Sioux will remain in the area?" She found coziness under the blanket. The fire also provided a soothing atmosphere to match the twinkling stars above them.

"This place once belonged to them until your people arrived, so I am told. Of course, they want their territory back. You are at war."

Alma shivered. Perhaps her destiny did lie with helping her ancestors fight the Dakota. According to the history she'd learned through her band, the Sioux Nation consisted of three main tribes—the Dakota, Nakota, and Lakota. The Ojibway had won against the Dakota, driving them deep into southern Minnesota, which pushed the Lakota to the Great Plains of the USA. Her people had even migrated to the prairies in Manitoba. Edie had mentioned that was where those who'd survived the Dakota attack had gone.

"Yes, we are at war." She gazed at him. "Maybe I was called here."

"Called here? You told me you came to save me."

"Maybe that was what got me here."

He frowned. "*Ma chérie*, you think too much."

"My sister said you call all the girls by that name."

He grinned. "Your sister has told you much about me."

"The more she spoke about you, the more I felt like I knew you."

"Tell me why she shared so much with you?" He set his elbow on his knee and settled his chin on his knuckles, his stare teasing.

"Maybe I asked her about you."

"Ah, you were curious, hmm?"

"Can you blame me? My sister, well, you know what she did."

He nodded, rubbing his chin, a task he seemed to perform whenever he was thinking.

Alma cocked her head. "You still do not believe me?"

"I find your story hard to fathom, that is all." The light from the fire played across his handsome face, the shadows falling into the hollows of his cheeks and highlighting the tip of his nose and smooth forehead.

"I guess it would be. If you showed up where I originally came from, telling me you are a French fur trader, I would also think you were lying, even if I held the proof in my hand."

Crickets lent their music to the fresh air. Not a bad cricket sound, but a soothing one to accompany their talk.

When Charlot ran his thumb along the bottom of her chin, Alma held his tender stare. He leaned in and brushed his mouth along her lips. Her insides melted, seducing her into returning the soft kiss. It wasn't the sensual one she'd experienced at the lake, but a coaxing one, inviting her to join him.

Her breathing increased.

Giddiness fluttered in her belly.

He really knew how to draw a woman into his dreams. When his tongue slipped between her lips, she met him halfway. His sensual taste of tobacco washed over her like the water in the lake. She leaned in, laying her hand over his shoulder.

The kiss deepened, his tongue lavishing hers with bold strokes. She sank deeper under his spell. If he'd been Ojibway, she would've likened him to a *jiisakii*, able to weave her into his good medicine, or leave her wondering if he'd used love medicine.

He cupped her cheek with his palm, the roughened skin producing goosebumps on her flesh. She could kiss him forever. With lazy strokes, his tongue rolled around hers, sucking the air from her lungs.

Her nipples hardened. The familiar heat she experienced while naked at the lake reappeared. Her body demanded she melt herself against him, experience his muscles firsthand.

The sounds of their kissing tickled her insides. Sexy and sweet wrapped into one. She didn't think people did this back in the eighteenth century, but they apparently acted the same as people in the twenty-first century.

People were people, Edie had said, adding that the only difference was technology and their way of thinking. Too true. Charlot was a product of his time, believing women had their place, but she was showing him they could be so much more.

He accepted her as a warrior.

This must be why he wanted her.

He'd even done his best to reassure her that she'd had no choice but to shoot the Dakota.

The familiar nausea filled her stomach. Part of her yearned to race through the forest to try and escape the reality of what she'd done.

She must've cringed or something because Charlot's lids fluttered, and he stopped kissing her.

"What is it?" His question came as a whisper

"Nothing." She swallowed. "I...I'm slowly trying to get used to—"

"Get used to being here, and what life is for everyone who lives here?"

She nodded.

"Violence happens. It is a way of life out here." He kept palming her face, using his thumb to rub her jawline. "You cannot dwell on something you were powerless to stop. It is why I asked you to perform your dance. It is also why I took the scalp. This is a celebration. You defeated someone who meant to bring us harm. If not you, I would have killed him."

Her stomach tightened. She nodded, unable to break his stare.

"Do you not think I experienced the same feeling when I first had to take a life? I was younger than you are. But I wanted to live the life my father lived. He told me what I tell you now. There are options, though."

"Options?"

"Yes, options. The longer you remain out here, the more you will face the same situation."

"You mean killing?"

"I mean defending yourself. We did not go on the warpath."

He was right.

"No, we did not."

"But there might come a time when we will have to."

The saliva drained from her mouth.

"Are you prepared to do so? Because if you cannot, it is best you return to Montréal, or whence you came."

Where she came from... "But the Sioux surround the area where I come from."

"We found a way to get your sister home, even when they had surrounded the area."

"You mean you'd risk your life again?" She gasped. No way. Not a chance. Not after she'd traveled here to save him. She shook her head. "I will not allow that."

"Allow what?"

"For you to face death again. I told you it was why I came—to help you."

"I am glad you came." He ran his thumb along her chin.

"You are?" Her heart fluttered.

He nodded. "*Oui*. You are the first warrior woman I have met. I must confess, at first I was not sure what to make of you..."

"And now?" She gulped.

"I am most fortunate to have met you." His gaze bestowed the depth of his gratefulness.

"I am fortunate too. Very fortunate."

He claimed her mouth again, drawing her deep into his kiss.

Chapter Fourteen: Agony and Ecstasy

ALMA MELTED INTO THE kiss. This time, she was ready for him. She wanted him. She'd not deny herself what she secretly ached for.

Charlot's hand shifted from her face and glided along her neck. She tilted her head. He took what she offered, breaking the kiss to nibble her jawline with tender pecks. His suckling drew the air from her lungs.

As he moved them to lie on his blanket, Alma's head spun. The beating of her heart thumped loudly in her ears.

He kept offering tender kisses to her neck. Then he used his tongue to trace a path leading from her throat to the scooped neckline of her tank top.

She froze. Would the trail lead to...

He kissed the swell of her breasts.

Everything inside her went off like a loud boom—her heart, her lungs, and even her blood seemed to burst from her body. All from one damned kiss, a tickle above her tits. Her breathing grew out of control, leaving her no choice but to dig her nails into her side to try to calm down. But that didn't help. Her nipples stood proud, begging to be tasted for the first time.

He worked his way to what she secretly ached for, his tongue beginning a new path from the swell of her breasts to between them. She stiffened, fear coiling tight in her belly. But he didn't seem to notice her stiffening as he pushed the scooped neckline of her tank top down to investigate further under her shirt, his tongue now between her boobs, tasting the sensitive area.

She had no choice but to wrap her arms around him, drawing him snugger against her chest. He slipped the hem of her tank top from its burrowing spot inside her pants, allowing the fresh air to hit her stomach.

He was undressing her little by little.

The excitement bubbling inside her expanded just like the hardness against her thigh, a hardness coming from his pants.

It had to happen for sure this time.

Please don't let the Dakota show up.

She crossed her fingers, gaping at the top of Charlot's head while he kept sampling the area between her breasts. Driven by desperation, the urge to rip off her bra rose up.

He settled his palm on her bare stomach. Having his raw flesh against her sensitive skin created a hot need between her legs. She shivered, waiting and anticipating his next move. His fingers walked along her skin, moving closer to her bra. As he closed in, she held her breath, heart pounding.

Then what she'd waited for happened. He pushed up her bra, exposing her breast and cupped it with his palm.

Being touched in such an intimate way for the first time left her quaking. Her knees nearly gave out. But there was more. He slid his finger over her nipple, caressing the hard peak.

Shock blasted through her veins. His caress taunted, teasing her to spread her legs and open for...something. Anything to stop the torment her body was undergoing.

He kept toying with her nipple until he leaned in, his breath moistening the tip.

A roar filled her ears. She squeezed her eyes shut.

His lips brushed the peak, setting off a million jolts of electricity. Alma curled her fingers into his hair, holding on for dear life. As if by instinct, her back arched, offering herself up to him.

Craving more of him, she longed to remove her tank top and bra. She panted and she tried to wiggle out of the garments.

His licks sent tickles between her legs, again, demanding she spread her thighs for him. But with pants on...

His lips left her nipple, and she nearly groaned, but he didn't give her a moment of respite. He pressed his mouth on her stomach, his breath steaming her skin. The moisture left her trembling. With his tongue, he created a new trail along her abs, not stopping until his mouth rested above her navel.

He unsnapped the button on her pants.

She gasped.

"Interesting," he murmured, his words hot on her exposed skin. "Your garment is very interesting." He lowered the zipper. "I have never seen such closures before." He popped his head up.

The heat of his mouth no longer lingered on her flesh, and disappointment filled her belly

"Perhaps you are what you say you are." He dug his fingers into the waist of her pants and gently tugged.

She wiggled her hips to ease their removal.

"These are quite lovely." He fingers lingered over her cotton panties.

Having him comment on something so intimate left Alma's face hot. She almost giggled, yet she found his fascination with her underwear sexy. Especially the way he stroked her through the cotton material. He kept drawing his finger up and down where her pussy lay hidden, as if anticipating what he'd do next.

She'd never expected her first time to be this much of an awakening, not with the guys she'd known back home. But again, she had to remind herself that twenty-six was a whole different age in this timeline. He was in the prime of his life, carefree in the wilderness. Was he ready for a wife and family?

Her mouth dried.

Wife.

Family.

In this century, at eighteen, she'd be ready for a husband and children, too.

Charlot pressed his lips against the cotton material covering her pussy. The heat from his mouth tightened the knots in her belly, and she bordered on exploding. Everything he did and said coaxed her to submit to the pleasure he was giving her.

She traced the rim of her mouth with her tongue, waiting for what her friends had exclaimed about when guys went down to their forbidden spots.

He hooked his fingers into the elastic waist of her panties, and she bit her lower lip and closed her eyes, doing her best not to cry out. He was too near... Too close... When he wormed his hand under the material, claiming the spot that only she had ever touched before, her breath came faster.

She couldn't hold back the moan that blasted from her throat. The heat between her thighs, where he dared to explore, wanted to spread like wildfire. Yet she yearned for him to delve further.

He teased her pubic hair, running his finger over the sensitive area. A *mmm* came from him, sounding as if he was licking his lips with delight. She didn't dare look and kept her eyes squeezed shut as he slipped her panties down her hips, leaving them at her thighs.

Was he studying her? Staring?

Part of her was mortified at being so exposed, the other delighted.

He pressed his face into her crotch, and she almost bolted straight up but forced herself to remain still as his breaths heated her pussy. He nuzzled the area, as if taking in her scent.

Wait. He was.

Shit, she'd never had a man sniff her before. What she found exciting was how much she enjoyed what he'd done.

His mouth skimmed her pubic hair, leaving steamy heat on her crotch. She swallowed, heart full of anticipation. His silky lips made contact, causing her to almost jump, astounded at the lushness of his kiss in such an intimate spot that made her body scream with joy.

She ached to wiggle from her sticky underwear so she could part her thighs, but Charlot kept kissing the area, even bestowing a pucker to the mound of hair above her slit. Blood raced through her veins, and she again curled her fingers into fists.

He flicked his tongue at the wet hairs of her pubic region.

This time, she strained to sit up, unable to ignore the mystery. She wanted to witness what was happening. When his tongue licked her slit, she about died, unsure if what she saw or what she felt was responsible for the jittering pleasure unfolding inside her. It was the hottest and most potent feeling she'd ever experienced—the kind that sweet-talked her into lying back to take in the pleasure.

His tongue slipped between her slit.

A heady sensation washed over her as his slow licks stroked her from the top of her mound to the crevice leading to her bottom.

"I need to…" She panted.

He peeked up from between her thighs.

Part of her yearned to tell him not to stop, to keep doing what he was doing.

"I know what you need, *ma chérie*. Lift your beautiful *derrière*."

Hearing him refer to her buttocks in such an intimate way left Alma gasping. She obeyed and flexed her hips.

He tossed aside her panties. "Perfect."

Above them, an owl hooted. The water lapped on the rocks. They were deep in nature, about to do what people had done from the beginning of time.

The pulsating between her thighs became more intense.

"Wrap your legs around my shoulders," Charlot cooed.

She shuddered but obeyed.

He buried his head back between her thighs, his breath dusting her pubic region with moist heat. She skimmed her fingers through his hair, electrified by the softness of each golden-brown strand, his velvety locks as sensual as his delicious licks between her pussy lips.

Nothing had prepared her for such pleasure. The more Charlot swirled his tongue around her sensitive area, the more the hairs on her arms stood at attention. Her insides squealed with anticipation. She raised her hips to grind in the same rhythm as his tasting.

Her excitement kept building. She tugged on his hair, needing to do something since the erotic sensations were coming at her too fast, trying to find a way out. Suddenly, an explosion tore through her, creating the most euphoric experience she'd ever undergone. She locked her thighs tighter around him, reveling in the ecstasy.

She opened her mouth, shocked at the exquisite sensations. Yes, she'd heard other girls speak about it, but nothing had prepared her for what an orgasm really felt like.

Charlot rose up, gaze intense.

She stared back, trying to catch her breath.

"I am going to claim you as mine," he whispered, pecking her cheek.

He fumbled with his belt, and his knuckles brushed against her stomach.

Instead of nervousness, longing crashed through Alma's veins, the need to feel him inside of her.

He lowered his pants.

The tip of warm flesh brushed against her pubic hairs.

She wrapped her legs around him, more than ready to take him, even though her heart screamed with a newfound fear. But she wasn't going to lose out on this moment, no matter how much she trembled.

Charlot leaned over her, his breath warm against her neck. The tip of his cock continued to feather the mound of her pussy. She raised her hips, and much to her shock, the head of his erection pressed on her opening.

This was it.

There was no turning back.

Nor did she want to turn back.

He was fully over her, staring deep into her eyes. Overwhelmed by his presence, she kept her attention firmly fixed on him. He brought his mouth down on hers, delving his tongue between her lips.

The tip of his cock breached her slowly.

When a sudden wave of pain shocked her system, she squeezed her eyes shut.

He murmured soothingly against her ear. "Easy, *ma chérie*. Yes, it will hurt, but only for a moment."

He remained still, waiting.

She drew in a breath, allowing her body to absorb the discomfort between her legs that was a far cry from what she'd experienced only moments ago with his tongue.

He brushed her cheek with his lips, soothing and relaxing her. The peacefulness helped. His girth had stretched her more than she expected. Yet having him claim her, as he'd promised, conjured up another round of excitement.

She once again wrapped her legs around him.

He moved slowly at first, giving her a small taste of his length. She arched her back, her pussy demanding she take in more of him. He plunged deeper, as if sensing her need.

As he rutted quicker between her legs, his kisses steamy on her neck, she lost herself in the pure rapture of the moment. Nothing had prepared her for the euphoria awakening in her soul. Just as he moaned, she also soared far away from the earth, drawn into pure bliss.

Chapter Fifteen: Heal My Soul

CHARLOT LAY SILENT atop Arms Oneself, struggling to catch his breath. The more he got to know her, the more her bravery drew him to her. Even now, she'd been afraid to engage in their joining, but once again she'd called on her courage. A man she'd only known two evenings.

He rose up on his elbow and gazed down. Not a hint of pink graced her cheeks. Instead, she stared back.

She ran her tongue across her lower lip.

He was ready to have her again after watching what seemed to be an invitation. "How are you feeling? Are you sore?"

She nodded.

Not a hint of regret lingered in her eyes, much to his relief.

Maybe the women from the place she stated to be from were more progressive, not caring to save their innocence for marriage. Then again, he'd bedded his share of *Saulteur* women who enjoyed hanging around the forts.

"It will pass," he reassured her. "It is the first time you have been breached. The more you engage in the act, the better you will feel afterward."

"Who says I do not feel good now?" A hint of sassiness lurked in her reply.

He should've known better.

"And...the act?" A twinkle in her eyes matched her voice.

"What would you like me to call it?"

She set her finger on her lower lip. "I guess there isn't a better word other than *coupling*."

"Coupling?" He arched a brow.

"Yes. It sounds nice."

"What do you call it where you come from?"

Her face reddened. "Let us not worry about what to call what we did. There are too many names for it."

"Ah..." He smiled at the evidence of her innocence but refused to tease her further.

He should rise, but the thought of leaving her warm body left a hint of disappointment in his chest. If he visited a widow, he usually enjoyed spending the night with the lovely lady cradled in his arms. But Arms Oneself wasn't a widow. She might not be comfortable sharing a sleeping mat. As for maidens, they ducked away and sneaked back to their parents' lodge.

The fire continued to crackle, giving off a good amount of smoke to keep the mosquitoes at bay.

"So this is how you couple?" Amusement lurked in her tone. "Cajole a maiden into bed and then engage in talk afterward?"

For an innocent to be so bold... Although he shouldn't be surprised that Arms Oneself found their moment amusing.

"Why do you ask?"

"I am simply curious, that is all. What happens next?"

"Perhaps I take you into my arms and we lie together...sleeping."

"I would like that." Shadows played over her face from the flickering fire, giving her bronze skin a warm glow.

"Then share my bedroll. Come." He patted the blankets.

ALMA'S HEART SEEMED to lodge in her throat. Not only had Charlot taken her virginity, but he wanted to share his bedroll. Excitement shimmied along the goosebumps peppering her arms.

She slid onto his blankets, nestling against the pit of his arm.

"Care to share a pipe?" His soft question caressed her skin.

"Yes."

"Then let me get us one."

She shifted so he could rise. As he leaned over to grab the pipe from their bundle of supplies, she peeked at his bare form. After being introduced to sex, she couldn't believe she craved more. Maybe everyone felt this way? Or was Charlot the reason for her desires?

He turned, holding out the pipe and some tobacco.

She stifled her giggle because their postcoital snuggle reminded her of the old-school movies Grandma loved to watch, when the couple would share a cigarette after sex.

Charlot nestled up against her, the warmth from his skin heating her flesh. He stuffed the pipe, his grin saying he more than enjoyed having her close.

In her excitement, she couldn't resist leaning her head on his shoulder. She'd never slept the entire night beside a man. If Mom were here, she'd toss a fit. But Mom wasn't. And Alma wasn't living in the twenty-first century, still called the dreaded *kid* word by older adults. Here, Charlot regarded her as a woman.

Mom...

Alma's heart suddenly ached for home. Did her parents miss her? Were they searching for her?

Wait.

Nobody had noticed Edie's absence when she'd insisted a whole year had passed after entering the corn maze, because she'd returned at the exact same time as when she'd first entered.

"You think too much." Charlot puffed on the pipe.

"I am thinking about home. Nothing more."

"Home? As in back east?"

No. Home was not back east. But there was no point in rehashing the truth. They'd just get into the same debate again. She merely shrugged.

"What you must think about out here is survival. I have lost most of my supplies. What I must do now is recoup."

She stiffened. "You mean returning to the village? The Dak—err, Sioux are probably still there."

"No. That would be foolish. Look around you..." With his hand still holding the pipe, he motioned at the vast wilderness surrounding them. "This is how I will recoup."

"Once you are healed...that is." Disappointment lay heavy in her chest. Hearing him say *I* instead of *we* clearly indicated he wished for her to return so he could continue being a lone trapper.

Well, why had she been having doubts? Or even daring to contemplate staying? She had a life and a family who'd miss her. She had her schooling to finish. And she was tired of speaking Ojibway, even though the lyrical words should be her first language.

This is all bullshit.

———— ✿ ————

97

WHEN ARMS ONESELF'S muscles stiffened, Charlot tensed. He had apparently said something to offend the raven-haired beauty, but he knew not what. Since he never had a lover or stayed anywhere long enough to court a maiden, he couldn't figure out what he had said to upset her.

Ah, women.

They were all the same.

This was why he'd chosen to remain single.

Between his sisters and mother, and the lovely women he'd bedded, they all made silent demands a man was supposed to know instinctively. Yes, he had great instincts, but not when it came to reading another's thoughts.

Here he'd assumed they'd enjoy a lovely night together.

"Perhaps we should eat. I could spear us some fish," he suggested, needing to do something to dispel the awkward moment Arms Oneself had turned their coupling into.

"It is dark out. We cannot see the fish," she murmured, although she gazed off at nothing.

The flatness of her voice indicated she continued to think about something that was upsetting her. Charlot stifled his sigh. So much for trying to rise and avoid this now uncomfortable spell. Still, he could find them something to eat. He began to sit up.

"What are you doing?" Alma's eyes flickered with unease, her lips pressed in a thin, wary line.

Perhaps getting up was a bad idea. Charlot's rumbling stomach could wait until the morning when he had a doubt-filled maiden on his hands. "I was going to extinguish my pipe," he lied.

Suspicion filled her gaze.

He'd best lay back down beside her or they might engage in another battle of wills, and he really didn't want to do that, not after what they'd shared. "Let us get some rest. We have much to do on the morrow. Such as fishing for some food."

She nodded.

He pulled her close against him, and she rested her head on his shoulder. When her breathing became deep and even, and her body relaxed, he continued to stare up at the night sky, shrouded in black ink since the simmering fire still gave off light.

His mind whirled around the woman in his arms. Her mercurial temperament always kept him on edge, but there was something irresistibly captivating about her presence. There was never a dull moment with Arms Oneself since she constantly kept him guessing, and maybe that wasn't so bad.

But just as Fire Woman proved she wasn't made for this land by disappearing back into the dancing flames, the same might be said for Arms Oneself. They were safe for now, but that wouldn't always be the case. Danger lurked everywhere in the wild. She belonged with her family back east, where civilization kept people safe.

Could he let her go, though?

Simply take her to the dancing flames and watch her disappear?

He'd already watched one leap from his life.

Now another might slip away.

A WET SNOUT WOKE ALMA. Followed by licks. She didn't have to open her eyes to know the bothersome pest was Theodore. He smelled of whatever he'd eaten when hunting for breakfast.

She opened her eyes to see her dog staring at her. "I know," she mumbled. "It is time to wake."

The fire had died down to nothing. As for the stickiness on her skin, a bath would help wash away the grime, along with the chilly morning dew.

"Come." She scooted out from beneath the blankets.

She gasped at her nakedness. Shit, she'd forgotten about going to sleep without any clothes on.

She glanced at Charlot, who continued to lightly snore, mink lashes on display.

Her fingers yearned to reach out and touch him, but she restrained herself. She had a busy morning because he wanted to continue traveling south to the fort, a place she'd visited many times in the twenty-first century as a replica.

She gathered up her clothes and quickly dressed. First, a fire was imperative, then she'd get them food, so the bath could wait. She stirred up the coals. When the glowing embers brightened, she added a bit of kindling. The small nest flamed, and she added more wood. Once the fire crackled, she whistled for Theodore to follow.

Right about then, she could use a cup of coffee. Maybe a Tim Horton's. But the famous Canadian coffee chain didn't exist yet. Did coffee even exist? Shit, did Canada exist, or was the country of the eighteenth century called something else? Maybe. Maybe not. At least Montréal was established.

She knelt at the rocky shoreline and splashed water on her face. It helped, but her icky body yearned to dive in head first. There had to be a way to make some kind of shampoo, too. If she recalled correctly, Great-Grandpa had mentioned cedar, which was abundant in this area. She'd ask Charlot how to make a hair-washing remedy from the delicious-smelling tree.

Thedore jumped into the water.

"Lucky you," she muttered. "I'll join you once I catch something."

And she succeeded. She caught four fish while Charlot continued to sleep. When she returned to the campfire, he sat up, rubbing his eyes.

"Good morning." He stared at the fish. "You have been busy, I see."

Funny, how nobody asked *what time is it* out here. She almost wanted to laugh. Probably because nobody wore a watch.

"Very busy. We need to eat our morning meal."

"I must say I never slept so well. I do not think I woke once, and I usually do." He rubbed his chin.

Hmm, that gesture meant he was thinking. Maybe about what they did last night?

Hope pattered in the same rhythm as Alma's heart. "Can you start the cooking? I need to bathe."

"Bathe?" Charlot's eyes widened. "But you bathed the other day."

Maybe people didn't clean every day in the eighteenth century. Yuck. "I will only be a moment. Theodore is already swimming."

"Ah yes, your dog." Charlot's gaze wandered to the lake.

A wave of nausea washed over Alma as she waited, Charlot's silence stretching between them like a taut wire. How were people supposed to behave after they'd done the deed?

Doing her best not to let her shoulders sag with melancholy, and ensuring she walked with a firm gait instead of dragging her feet, she headed for the lake, many steps from the campfire.

She stood at the rock leading into the water glistening under the sun and removed her clothing. Just as she submerged herself, the leaves from a bush rustled.

Theodore bared his teeth, growling. He swam further in, moving closer to the shore.

"Easy, boy, it's just Charlot." Her crushed hope bloomed brighter than a flower. She turned her head, gasping.

The person emerging from the bush wasn't Charlot, but another French fur trader. She stifled her scream and quickly covered herself, making sure every bare spot was hidden except for her head.

The bearded man eyed her, a dirty-looking stranger who needed a washing more than her. He held a musket. A contraption of some kind, which he probably used as a backpack, rested on his back.

Thedore bounded from the water, barking.

Chapter Sixteen: Stranger in the Dark

SUDDEN BARKING SHATTERED the quiet, sending a chill racing down Charlot's spine. The dog was noisy for just one reason. He snatched up his musket and stood since he'd been hunched over the fire cooking the fish he'd filleted. Thank goodness he always kept his weapon loaded.

As he darted to where the dog kept barking, much to his relief, his side did not produce the insufferable ache as it had the previous day. A good night's rest had done him well.

He broke through the bush and froze.

Another trapper stood on one of the big rocks leading into the lake.

The man whipped around and crouched, musket ready in his hands. Then his eyes brightened in recognition, and he stood straight.

Charlot frowned. Pierre Lacroix. He'd met the man at the fort a few times. They weren't well acquainted, but they were polite whenever they crossed paths. He never had intentions of befriending Pierre, though, for his reputation did not sit well with the *Saulteurs*.

"I smelled your fire last night," Pierre offered. "I thought you were Indians, but I see you are keeping one Indian." His thick lips formed a salacious grin.

"She is with me. My traveling companion."

Theodore stood on the rock, his growls low, putting himself between Arms Oneself and Pierre.

"Is this her dog?" Pierre asked.

"Yes. Speak in their language. She does not understand French."

Pierre glanced back at Arms Oneself, who continued to hide in the water, covering her naked flesh.

A hint of arousal stirred in Charlot's pants, but annoyance also surfaced. "Give the woman a moment to cover herself. Come." He used the butt of his musket to motion from whence he came. "My apologies for the disturbance," he offered to Arms Oneself. "Please, continue with your bathing. I am cooking us our morning meal."

Arms Oneself nodded, her cheeks flushed.

Charlot waited for Pierre to move first. The big man grudgingly stalked off the rock and swaggered toward the scent of the fire.

"This is the first I have known you to take a woman along." A slyness tinged Pierre's tone.

"She is the daughter of a chief," Charlot lied. "I am escorting her to her family."

Pierre's shoulders tightened, something Charlot had hoped would happen, since this told the man Arms Oneself was a woman of importance and had a family of even greater importance—though with the *Saulteurs*, all were equal.

The French revered such positions within their own culture, and most assumed every other race did as well. After living amongst the Indians for so long, Charlot knew the *Saulteur* people did not think in such terms.

"Which band does she belong to?" Pierre sat on a stump by the fire.

"He Paddles Fast," Charlot lied again, a chief he'd heard of, but never sat and broke bread with before. The chief's people lived south of here. He made sure to turn the fish before they burned.

"Ah, I see." Pierre eyed the food.

To not offer something was considered rude, so Charlot forced himself to say, "Will you join us?"

"I am famished, but I passed on eating since I wanted to explore who the fire belonged to. All has been quiet out here. I did not expect anyone else."

"It is always quiet now. The Indians are at their lake homes, busy with their summer villages, gathering what they will need to survive another winter."

Pierre tapped his cheek. "Yes, this is when they do their fishing. They love the *esturgeon*."

"As do I." Charlot glanced toward the bush but saw no sign of Arms Oneself.

"She's a rather plain woman, but out here, any woman will do, hmm?" Pierre snickered. "A man does get lonely... A woman offers much comfort during the night."

An edge of defensiveness swamped Charlot. He made sure to keep his words light. "As I said, she is the chief's daughter. I do not view her in any other way. I am aiding her and nothing more."

Still, the insult stung. Arms Oneself may not be a raving beauty like her older sister, but she was far from plain. Her determination, stubbornness, and skill produced beauty unique to her, along with her smooth skin, lack of proper decorum, and big searching eyes.

Yes, only she would trudge off to bathe naked in the lake, unaware of what lurked in the bushes. Now she knew of the true dangers out there, and all were not animals.

ALMA DONNED THE LAST of her clothing. She sniffed. Besides scrubbing her skin, she should have washed her pants and tank top as well. What would the stranger think of her apparel? She needed to buy something at the fort to blend in here. The man might not think she was a lady if she arrived at the campsite in what was deemed as men's clothing.

With Theodore at her side, she scooped up her rifle and started for the fire, belly rumbling. When she emerged from the bushes, pushing aside a branch from a spruce tree, she found Charlot and the man seated, eating the fish she'd caught. Her meal rested on the rocks. The man used the spare plate, and Charlot had been kind enough to keep hers at the fire.

"Your meal awaits." Charlot used his chin to motion at her food. He had pierced his fish with a stick so he could eat.

"You are the daughter of He Paddles Fast, I hear." The man spoke in a heavy French accent. His voice was low but not gruff. His golden-brown eyes studied her carefully.

Being under his scrutinizing gaze elicited a hint of annoyance in Alma. She should be flattered to have the attention of a handsome man, but there was something about this one she did not trust, plus her dog's ear remained flat and his hackles raised.

She glanced at Charlot, clearing her throat. "Yes."

"This is Pierre Lacroix. He traps in this area." Charlot muttered the introduction, clearly not pleased.

Alma nodded.

"How were you separated from your family?" Pierre shoved the last of the fish into his mouth.

She again whipped her gaze at Charlot.

"You know how young women are. She desired to explore and became lost." Charlot shrugged.

Alma was no fool. Charlot thought of playing a game of unconcern. Whatever lie he'd told the strange man, she'd play along. Charlot thought to protect her or maybe protect her identity.

"Those are odd." The man pointed to her camouflage pants.

"They belong to my brother. I made them for him." Alma's cheeks heated.

"Hmm..." The man kept eyeing her pants.

Thank goodness she had kept her boots at the rocks, or he would've questioned those as well, since all natives wore moccasins.

"Did you wear out your moccasins?" The man now studied her bare feet.

"Yes. I need to make more when I reach the village." She set the tin plate on her lap.

Charlot cleared his throat, staring hard at Pierre.

Pierre at least had the appropriateness to flush.

Obviously, the stranger had produced a *faux pas* of some kind because Charlot continued to glare at him.

Maybe the man asked too many questions? Or perhaps he wasn't supposed to engage a maiden in conversation? Alma wasn't sure. She kept her head down in a demure manner, hoping it was how maidens of this time conducted themselves. Too bad she didn't study her ancestors the way Edie had.

The fire crackled. Charlot stared blankly into the flickering flames.

Alma snuck a look at the stranger, who also stared at the flames. Only the munching on their food provided noise, along with the chirps from the birds and other sounds of nature. Theodore sat by her side, also silent, his gaze fixed on the man.

For someone to happen upon them in the middle of nowhere seemed very strange. Or had the man deliberately sought them out? She snuck a peek at Charlot who had finished eating. He loathed company unless he sought others. He'd even given her grief when she'd first tried to help him. Perhaps he'd send the stranger packing once they'd eaten. They would be pulling up stakes quickly since he wanted to spend the day traveling to the fort.

"I can accompany you." Pierre arched a thick brow. "I see you are injured." He used his chin to point at Charlot's side.

"It is almost healed," Charlot replied. "I am fine."

"We are traveling in the same direction." Pierre used the back of his sleeve to wipe his mouth as he set aside the tin plate.

Charlot's jawline tightened. "I prefer to travel alone."

Pierre flashed a sly smile. "She is a maiden. Having me accompany you will ensure she is *safe* when we arrive at her village."

She assumed his emphasis on the word *safe* implied that people would believe nothing had happened between Charlot and Alma.

"True." Charlot tossed the stick he'd used to eat the fish with into the fire.

"I am sure you approve?" Pierre shifted his gaze to Alma.

What else could she do? If she was portraying one of her female ancestors, she would have to nod and remain polite. She'd supposedly shame this family they were taking her to if she behaved rudely.

Although she loathed to do so, she forced a smile at Pierre. Sure, he was handsome, but not near Charlot's league, maybe because there was something in the stranger's eyes that couldn't hide his malignant thoughts.

She rose to clean up. Theodore stayed by her side while she washed and packed up the camp, but he kept an eye on Pierre.

Once Alma had everything ready, she glanced toward her hidden rifle. Dammit, Pierre would see the weapon, and then there were her boots she still had to retrieve from the rocks.

"You may lead the way." Charlot made a sweeping motion with his hand. "I will cover the back."

Alma almost giggled at Charlot's cunning since he'd played to the stranger's ego. Pierre's smile reeked of arrogance as he positioned himself first.

"I will retrieve my other belongings." Before they could say anything, she bolted for the rocks where she'd left her boots. Theodore remained beside her.

Once she reached the place where she'd bathed, she sat on the rock to slip on her boots. Theodore stood guard close by.

"You are a good boy." She reached over and petted his silky fur. "I know I am safe here with you, but I do not trust the stranger. You do not either. Which means he is not a good person."

A low growl came from Theodore.

"You are right. We must keep a close eye on him. Especially tonight when we camp. I do not want him sneaking into my bedroll."

She stood, having donned her boots and tied the laces. "Let us hope he does not take too close a look. We might be able to trick him. Come."

She made her way back to the camp to find Pierre and Charlot waiting. The ankle-length grass hid her feet.

"Let us be on our way," Pierre announced.

Alma waited for Pierre to take his position. Once he faced forward, she reached for her rifle and backpack.

Charlot did not place her in the middle but fell in step behind Pierre, much to her relief.

They were off, not having to break through the underbrush since Pierre must have created a path when making his way toward their camp earlier. Theodore kept close to Alma, almost stepping on her heels.

The only noise came from their light footsteps as they did their best not to crush too much of the foliage they trekked through. The scent of moss and dewy leaves filled the air, a pleasant scent Alma usually enjoyed. Yet she found it hard to relish the glorious morning with a stranger in their midst.

Somehow, Charlot had to rid them of the man before they reached the village, or she'd have some major explaining to do when Pierre presented her to the chief.

They walked for almost an hour when Charlot called out, "Keep on going. The maiden must stop to answer nature's call."

Pierre never looked back but kept walking.

Charlot pivoted.

Alma gazed up at him. There was something in his eyes she could not read. Want? Need? Her legs quivered.

"This is your chance, *ma chérie*," he told her with a hint of regret in his tone. "You say you are born like this—to be a woman of the interior. Then you should not have a problem finding the dancing flames. You can return. I can find a way to stop him before we can follow you. We are taking a big risk now that he accompanies us."

Alma swallowed. Go back? "But you are not fully healed."

"I am healed enough." Firmness settled into his tone.

"I do not trust him. What if he does something to you?"

"He will not, for he has had many opportunities to do so. This is not the first time we have crossed paths," he reassured her. "If he wished death for me, he had many other chances to kill me. I worry he will learn what I have about you. There is also your weapon. If he sees it, he will *kill* for it."

The moisture in Alma's throat evaporated. Could she leave Charlot? She had accomplished the reason why she traveled back in time. To save him. He was saved.

He studied her, waiting.

She could say yes or no.

If she said no, she'd be taking a big risk continuing.

If she said yes, she'd never see Charlot again.

Chapter Seventeen: Power of the Night

"I WILL REMAIN." ALMA squared her shoulders. "As I said, I do not trust him."

A hint of a smile tugged at Charlot's pink lips. He raised his hand, as if he wished to brush his fingers along her hair. "You know I can more than handle him, injured or not. Do you think this is the first time I have been injured out here?"

Alma did her best not to bristle at his taunting tone. "I am aware you are more than capable of caring for yourself, but two is better than one, is it not?"

"Ah, true." Charlot wagged his eyebrows in a teasing manner. "Maybe you enjoy my company more than you care to admit, hmm."

Oh ho, he thought to become smug again? Maybe she should turn back? "If you wish me to leave..."

Shit, why had she made the threat? What if he said yes?

Seconds passed.

Alma held her breath as she stared down Charlot.

His eyes crinkled at the corners. He even tilted his head. "I am enjoying your company, warrior woman." He chuckled.

His light laughter danced along Alma's skin.

"Then we shall journey on. I think you also enjoy mine."

She bristled. "Enjoy your what?"

"My company. What else?" His gaze was as smug as his words. "Did you really think I would have allowed you to return to the dancing flames by yourself?"

Should she be flattered or insulted? The bastard had tricked her for the second time. The jerk had only said those words to see if she'd remain of her own accord. "I am not a weak woman like my sister, who needs the assistance of men." She thrust her chin out.

"No, you are not." Charlot grinned. "Come. We best get moving or Pierre will wonder about our absence." He pivoted, giving her his back as he led the way.

Grumbling under her breath, Alma followed.

They met up with Pierre a short while later and kept walking until the sun rose to high noon. A blanket covered her backpack at least, but she had no way to hide her rifle from a man who Charlot claimed would kill her for the weapon. Great, something she would soon have to deal with.

Maybe she should've taken off for the dancing flames. But would they even still be present? She could be stranded with an infuriating man who'd thought to test her, and to whom she'd given her virginity.

As annoyed and frustrated as she was, she couldn't stop admiring Charlot's backside and his natural gait. Even injured, nothing stopped him from navigating this wild wilderness.

Pierre stopped and turned to Charlot. "I think it is time we rest. A chance for some water and to smoke. What do you say?" He craned his neck, obviously looking for her.

"I agree. A rest is good." Charlot also stopped, blocking Pierre's view.

Alma couldn't wait to sit. Her feet hurt. She quickly plopped on a stump and removed her boots, hiding them under the blanket with her backpack before Pierre noticed. When she locked her fingers together and brought her arms over her head to stretch, the lusty Frenchman's gaze became hungry, as if watching his meal.

Alma quickly dropped her arms. She had no intention of being Pierre's lunch. When his gaze traveled to her bare feet, she shrugged.

It seemed horny men lurked everywhere, no matter the century.

Charlot handed over a water skin that Pierre had passed to him. "Drink up," he told her. "Once we leave, we will not stop again until nightfall."

They weren't near water, so she'd follow his order. She'd also give some to Theodore, who sat by her side.

Once she quenched her thirst, she removed a bowl from her backpack and poured some water for Theodore. "Drink up. I am sure you need some."

Pierre, who'd sat back against a tree, sputtered. "What are you doing? It is a dog."

"He is *my* dog." Alma set the bowl in front of Theodore. "He needs this as much as we do."

Pierre slapped his hand against his forehead, muttering something Alma could not hear. He was probably mumbling that her people placed too much importance on animals. Stupid man.

Charlot offered up his pipe.

Alma gladly took a drag, letting the smoke curl down her throat, which released the tension in her shoulders. Maybe there was a way they could ditch Pierre. She glanced at Charlot, who waited for her to return the pipe to him.

Pierre had stood, hands on his hips, facing away from them.

She leaned toward Charlot. "We must leave him in the middle of the night," she whispered. "He cannot learn I am not the daughter of a chief."

Charlot nodded.

They rose

Pierre swiveled to face them. "We should be off. It will be an all-day walk before we reach my camp."

"Very well." Charlot picked up his musket.

While the men strode ahead, Alma used the spare moment to re-don her boots. She followed with Theodore bringing up the rear.

The constant heat, black flies nipping at Alma's exposed skin, and the leaves brushing at her—probably covered in ticks—became a battle of wills. She had trekked through the wilderness many times, but not for this long, or during high afternoon.

She reassured herself by thinking that Edie never would've survived this trek.

Alma frowned.

She'd spent her whole life comparing herself to Edie. She silently vowed to stop. This was a different time and place. Here, she was Arms Oneself. Did Edie go through life bothered by Alma's thoughts? No. Only fools allowed their insecurities to live rent-free inside their heads. She wouldn't do so anymore. Charlot had helped her see she had special gifts of her own, even if he did mock her now and again.

She'd more than proven she could endure where her older sister had stumbled.

Alma thrust out her chin and drew back her shoulders. Big deal if she was Charlot's second pick. She wouldn't see him after this adventure. Once she returned to the twenty-first century, she'd find someone who liked her for her looks, not because she was the only available woman. That was, of course, after she realized her goals, whatever those might be. Maybe she'd find them in this century.

Instead of sitting inside an office, perhaps she could work in the field of sports and recreation, teaching the youth about wilderness survival?

DUSK HAD FALLEN WHEN they neared Pierre's camp, which was inundated with an endless swarm of mosquitoes. They'd have to build a fire, and fast, before they were eaten alive.

Pierre stopped and pulled a birch bark container from his pack. "I have some bear grease." He coated himself in the stuff and then handed the concoction to Charlot.

"Ladies first," Charlot said as he offered up the container.

"*Meegwetch*." Alma wouldn't argue. The pests were treating her like an all-you-can-eat buffet. Once she lathered up her exposed body parts, she rubbed down Thedore's ears, nose, and snout with the stuff. The mosquitoes wouldn't be able to get through his furry parts.

She ignored Pierre's snort since he probably believed animals didn't deserve precious bear grease. Well, hers did.

When they finally reached the spot situated near a lake, she let out a big sigh. Pierre even had a hut built for his trapline. At least they could sleep inside, get some rest before they vanished in the middle of the night.

Much to Alma's annoyance, Pierre suggested she cook, no doubt because she was a damned woman. Instead of settling inside the cabin, she used the outside campfire to make them another meal of fish. She gaped at Pierre's stockpile of blueberries, raspberries, wild onions, mushrooms, and other treats to add to their meal, along with herbs. She gave him an acknowledgement for his gathering supplies to see him through the winter.

Once she finished cooking, they ate outside. The smoke from the fire kept the mosquitoes at bay. Theodore settled by her side, belly full of fish.

Pierre had a good spot. His hut wasn't *on* the lake, but set further into the interior, yet close enough to break the ice to retrieve water in the winter while trapping.

"You picked a good spot." Unsure what had possessed her to compliment the stranger, which received raised eyebrows from Charlot, Alama simply shrugged her shoulders.

Pierre's full lips spread into his usual smug grin. "*Merci*. I have been out here for a long time. I favor this spot for its proximity to the lake and the animals I trap."

He munched on a bit more fish before looking up from his plate. "Tell me, why did you leave your home?"

Alma cleared her throat. She'd give the same excuse she identified with in the future. "I prefer to be a warrior."

Pierre snickered. "A warrior?"

"There are female warriors amongst my people." Alma didn't hide the defensiveness in her voice.

Charlot looked up to the darkening sky, as if ready to sigh.

"You have no desire to marry then?"

"No." Why was everyone so intent on marriage in this century? "A woman can fend for herself."

"Not out here. This is why your kind gather in bands, am I not correct? To be alone means death," Pierre pointed out.

"You are alone out here. So is Monsieur Baudelaire."

"Ah, you do not call him by his Christian name?"

"Is this not improper?" Alma arched a brow. Score one for her, she was playing this game well.

"True, unless you are extremely well acquainted or...intimate." Pierre waggled his brows.

Alma drew up, doing her best to appear offended. "I am a maiden."

"Yes, you are." Pierre pursed his lips. "Yet you also wish to be a warrior. I believe those breeches do not belong to your brother. I believe they belong to you."

Stifling the growl ready to erupt, Alma squared her shoulders. "Breeches are much more practical out here."

"You wish to live the life of a *berdache*?"

What the hell was that? "No. I wish to live the life of a woman."

"Hmm..." Pierre scratched his cheek. "You are a strange one." He stood. "I need my pipe. Already night has come. We have a long trip tomorrow."

Alma cleared her throat. Maybe they wouldn't have to sneak away. "Why not remain here. Monsieur Baudelaire knows the way to my village. He can continue to accompany me."

Pierre gave another of his dumb, sly grins. "Ah? You do not worry about your reputation and wish to travel with him alone?"

Alam gritted her teeth. "I do not wish to inconvenience you. I am sure you have much to prepare for the winter."

"There is no inconvenience," he assured her.

She stood to shut down the conversation. They'd have to sneak off in the middle of the night after all.

While the men enjoyed their pipes, she busied herself with cleaning up their meal. Normally, she'd loathe being left with the task, believing they'd given her the responsibility because she was a woman. This time, she didn't care since she could avoid Pierre's nosey questions, which bordered on figuring out the truth.

She packed away some stuff into her backpack, being careful Pierre could not spy on her because he'd know her rifle and supplies were not of this century.

Pierre stood and went inside the tiny cabin. He returned, pointing a flintlock pistol at Charlot. "I believe everything you have told me is a lie. She is not the chief's daughter. No daughter would disgrace a father of importance the way the girl has. I think she ran off from another band with you."

Charlot set down the pipe.

Alma scrambled for her rifle, heart pounding so loudly that she could almost hear the beating in her ears. Fear and anger raced through her veins, and blood rushed to her head.

"You think to kill me?" Charlot stood, steps away from where he'd set down his musket.

Alma's mouth dried. Last time she had to take the life of the Dakota warrior to save Charlot. Now she was being tested again. Could she take this man's life, too?

Chapter Eighteen: Prelude to Madness

ALMA RELEASED THE SAFETY of her rifle and aimed. Maybe she wouldn't have to kill the traitor Pierre. Wounding him could suffice. "Put down your weapon."

Much to her shock, when Pierre turned to look her way, Charlot hurled himself at the bigger man.

The shout lodged in her throat came close to escaping, but she swallowed the lump and remained silent. There was no way she would distract Charlot. He needed his full attention.

Theodore growled, ready to spring forward.

"Stay," she warned the dog.

Someone was going to get killed if they kept wrestling for the gun.

Charlot had seized Pierre's wrist, shaking it to get the man to drop the weapon. But Pierre kept pushing forward, attempting to get Charlot off balance. Charlot ground in his heels, again launching himself at Pierre. The impact sent both men tumbling to the ground.

Alma tried to keep the sights of her rifle trained on Pierre as they rolled around in the dirt, closing in on the fire. If she did not fear for Theodore's life, she'd send him into the battle to attack Pierre, but the bastard might shoot her dog.

Charlot climbed on top of Pierre, still wrestling for the pistol. Just as Charlot secured his fingers around Pierre's wrist, Pierre grabbed a handful of sand and tossed it into Charlot's face. Charlot let out a strangled cry, his fingers swiping where the sand had hit his eyes.

Pierre raised his pistol...

Theodore pounced, barking, barreling for Pierre...

Alma fired her rifle...

A roar filled her ears as the horrid scene continued to unfold in front of her. Just as she'd taken down the Dakota warrior without hesitation, she'd done the same thing again. Pierre slumped to the ground with Charlot still on top of him.

Charlot snapped his head up, gaping.

With trembling hands, Alma lowered her rifle. "He...he was going to kill you." Even her teeth clattered.

This was awful.

Horrible.

How could she return to her family after killing two men?

The rifle clattered to the ground.

She covered her face with her hands.

"*Ma chérie*," Charlot whispered.

His scent filled Alma's nose, and she didn't have to expose her face to know he stood close to her. Charlot wrapped his arms around her waist and drew her against his chest.

She cradled her head on his shoulder. "I can never go back now. Never. Not after—"

"What have I told you already?" he murmured.

He'd told her killing was a part of life out here. Danger lurked everywhere. Warriors only murdered in retaliation, for vengeance, and to defend themselves. She thought of herself as a warrior, but right then, she felt as fragile as her sister.

Wait.

Edie wasn't fragile.

She'd fought hard and did her best to adapt in this century. She'd even wanted to remain. If Alma asked the dreaded *what-would-Edie-do* question, would that make her weak? Incompetent? Another failure when compared to her sister?

Fine, she'd make her own decision, even with tears threatening to spill from her eyes. "We must bury him. We cannot leave him here."

"That we will do," Charlot reassured her. "If we do not, people will know he met a wrongful death. You can sleep while I begin digging a grave."

"No, I will help. I was the one who—"

He cupped her face in his hands, forcing her to stare at him. "Why do you argue so much? Why do you fear being looked upon as weak? Why are you determined to prove yourself?"

Alma stiffened. He was right. She was always on the defensive. Hadn't she decided she'd no longer let envy influence her? Edie had her life, and Alma had hers.

"I killed him. Therefore, I must bury him."

With his thumb, he traced her cheekbone. "You did what you had to do. Nobody told him to retrieve his pistol to attempt to kill me. If he had succeeded, we know what he would have done to you."

"I know." She couldn't bow her head since Charlot's thumb was under her chin, nor could she glance away. Instead, she held his stare.

"I will bury him while you rest."

He was right. Shock continued to reverberate through her body. Sleep would help. "Yes."

His lips spread into a wide smile. He kissed the tip of her nose.

The gentleness of his mouth on her skin spread warmth through her belly. Maybe he did care. "*Meegwetch*."

He stepped back.

Hugging herself, she shuffled into the small cabin to the bed of leaves.

"Come with me, dog. Let your mistress sleep. I will need your help," Charlot said.

Alma stopped, just about to lie down. He asked Theodore for help, but passed on hers? No, she wouldn't go outside and start another debate. He cared enough to ask her to sleep off her shock.

She cringed.

Dead.

Another dead by her hand.

A lump grew in her throat, and she didn't fight the tears gathering in the corner of her eyes this time. She crawled onto the bed, not caring that another had lain there, and lord knew if insects crept everywhere.

"*Ma chérie*," Charlot called out.

Alma rolled over.

Charlot held her sleeping bag. "I thought you might wish to use this."

His thoughtfulness touched her heart. Maybe he even held the quickly beating thing in his palm.

"Thank you."

"Sleep well. You have been through much." He brushed at her hair with a small smile. "I like that you wear it short."

Her heart swelled even bigger.

"It suits you." He pivoted and left the cabin.

She drew the sleeping bag over her, Pierre's dead eyes continuing to spook her like a ghost.

CHARLOT CUSSED UNDER his breath. That was the second time Arms Oneself interfered. Not interfered… Intervened. He understood she assumed he was in danger and wanted to help, but when would she allow him to help her?

He tied Pierre's feet to the rope he'd secured to the dog's contraption that had allowed the mighty beast to pull the travois. Taking the trapper further inland was imperative. He could not allow anyone to find Pierre's body, nor let the wolves uncover the corpse, for they'd smell the scent of death. He'd be digging all night, and praying the earth wouldn't collapse in while making Pierre's grave.

Thedore proved his powerful strength by pulling the man along the ground, following Charlot's trail as he pushed aside the underbrush. In the summer, the woods grew thick. Too thick. But he stayed clear of the animal trails. Animals meant wolves sniffing out deer to hunt, and a deep grave did not guarantee they wouldn't smell Pierre's corpse.

He stopped at a spot hidden in the underbrush, a perfect place to hide a fresh grave until nature did its job by covering the mound in grass.

Too bad the dog couldn't dig for him, but he stuck the shovel into the earth and began the process. With Arms Oneself's beloved pet watching, he spent most of the night tossing aside dirt to ensure the grave proved deep enough to lay Pierre in. Even though the scoundrel didn't deserve it after attempting to kill him, Charlot wrapped the man in one of their precious blankets, which left him no choice but to purchase a new one at the fort. As much as he loathed the man, the human side of him couldn't simply toss Pierre into the hole without some kind of dignity.

He swiped at the sweat along his brow.

Theodore gazed up at him.

"We are finished, my friend," he said in French. "Come. Let us see how your mistress is doing."

Carrying the shovel, he trudged back to the small cabin with the dog following. Since Pierre had stocked the lodge, Charlot wouldn't have to fish for breakfast. Perhaps they could also pack as much as they could into that strange contraption Arms Oneself carried on her back. Even load the dog with more of the essentials.

It was a pity they could not remain here, but to do so meant implicating themselves in Pierre's whereabouts, for someone would notice the trapper's disappearance in time.

Charlot couldn't lie and say Pierre had returned to Montréal, for the waterways operated the same as the moccasin trail—people learned sooner or later of incidents that had occurred. There could even be talk. He could even be brought in to face the magistrate.

He entered the cabin, seeing Arms Oneself fast asleep, still curled up in her strange blanket. Part of him ached to crawl in and rest his weary body, but they had to make haste and pack whatever provisions they could claim.

Before he could lean down and wake her, Thedore stepped up on the padding of grass and leaves, nuzzling his mistress.

Arms Oneself stirred. "Teddy..." she murmured, draping her arm across the dog. "Let me sleep longer. I'm tired."

The language confused Charlot, but he was almost certain the words she had spoken in were English. Did she believe she was elsewhere?

"*Ma chérie*, we must pack and leave."

Her eyelids flickered, her face a bit puffy. "Oh." Her gaze moved from side to side as she sat up. "Yes, we will get packed."

Her pursed lips and furrowed brow revealed her sorrow.

He stifled his sigh. This was something she'd have to work out. He'd already talked to her about the dangers within the interior. "Rise."

He set his hands on his hips and glanced around. They'd take the food Pierre had gathered so far and some of the supplies. This would suffice until they found a place to settle. Maybe they'd make their way to *Rivière à la Pluie*. There were plenty of sturgeons there to fish—big, powerful beasts they could smoke. Since he'd lost his canoe at the village when the Sioux had attacked, he'd build another one there.

"Where are we going?" She stood behind him.

"The spirit rapids. A place your people call *Manidoo Ziibi*." He grabbed a sack and handed it over to her. "Pack the food, as much as you can stuff into that contraption you place on your back."

Once they had everything they needed, he led them out the door. "We can construct a lodge of our own once we reach the river."

Her cheeks reddened. "Our own?"

"*Oui*. Winter is coming. We must be prepared. I must trap."

She frowned. "Winter is a long ways away."

"We live by the seasons out here, and everything we do now is in preparation for the coldest time," he informed her. "There are two of us now. We must think about a lodge." She could also be carrying his child.

"Wait. What about the dancing flames?" She shimmied up behind him before they entered the underbrush.

"As I said, it is too risky now. We must wait. Especially now that Pierre is dead."

She winced.

"Do not look upset. We know what darkness lurked in his black heart. Come."

"Did you know him well?" She followed him into the bush.

Theodore joined them, dragging the travois with extra supplies.

"No. As I said, we were merely acquaintances. I did not trust him. Neither did your people. Not many trusted him. He was simply left to his own devices." Charlot used the end of his musket to move aside the thick brush.

He was truly mad for bringing Arms Oneself deeper into his life and the wilderness. Even worse, the thought she might be carrying his child didn't produce a shudder of shock, but one of calm. Perhaps he sought an excuse to keep her here? Maybe because he feared admitting to himself that he had no desire to see her leave.

When did this woman warrior find her way inside of him? How did she creep up when he wasn't looking to worm her way past his control?

He pushed on, shoving aside the thoughts. He had to take them to a safer place, far from the cabin...far from what had happened.

It was time to start something new. What that was, he didn't yet know.

Chapter Nineteen: She's in Love

ALMA'S HEART SKIPPED a beat, even though guilt continued to gnaw at her insides. Charlot wanted her to remain. He wished to find them a safe place where they could begin preparing for the winter.

When Theodore woke her, she initially believed she was at home in her own bed, experiencing a dream. But hearing Charlot's voice reaffirmed the awfulness of what had occurred earlier. His concern, and then his plan of heading for the very spot where she currently lived in the twenty-first century, made her heart swell.

As they trekked through the bush, she noticed Charlot didn't use a branch for a cane. She supposed he wouldn't have to after spending the night digging Pierre's grave.

Dammit, she didn't need a reminder about what she'd done. She understood she had no choice, but shooting a man, even if in self-defense, bothered her.

Wait. It shouldn't.

Pierre had clearly planned on killing Charlot and then raping her. Anger surfaced. Like hell she'd allow a man to rape her. Pierre Lacroix had been a first-rate fool. No more thinking about him. He didn't deserve her guilt. Instead, she'd concentrate on the present.

If she consulted Google Maps, the app would show that they were in store for a long journey to reach the Rainy River, the very place where her family lived. Or did Charlot plan on taking them further east or west of her family home?

"What about bark?" Great-Grandpa and Grandpa had told Alma the precious outer layer of the birch tree could only be peeled during a short window in the spring. They were well past the season.

"We can trade," Charlot assured her. "Plenty of your people have villages along the river."

"Trade with—" She cut herself off, realizing it was a silly question since they had plenty of Pierre's possessions.

Their journey could take a long time without a canoe. Alma wasn't nervous about running out of water since the lakes were plentiful in this area. Even small ones. And ponds.

Being deep in the interior raised the hair on her arms, though. She was used to being able to leave without incident. But she'd keep her fears from Charlot. Even having such fears annoyed her, but she couldn't deny they were present.

They walked all day, only stopping for a quick bite to eat before continuing. When Alma felt her legs would give out with another step, Charlot finally halted next to a huge open pond. A perfect place to refill their water carriers and make a fire to eat more of the food they'd taken from Pierre's hut.

Once they built a lean-to for shelter, Alma found a stump to sit on while Charlot tended the fire. The smoke would do them good. Already the mosquitoes were out, attempting to feed on their blood.

She ate some smoked meat, savoring each bite after a long day of walking with a heavy pack on her back.

Charlot sat on a fallen log. He placed his elbows on his knees, hat in hand, which he moved to and fro. "Get some sleep. It will be another long day tomorrow."

Sleep alone? Alma's chest tightened. She never knew where she stood with this man. Did he want her for a companion or what?

"Very well." She rose and reached for her backpack.

"I will keep watch for now."

She stiffened. "Keep watch for what?"

"We have a fire going. Anything could be out there."

He was right. Great. She'd forgotten the lesson her grandfather repeated often.

She laid out her sleeping bag. It'd be another long day traveling, so she'd best get her butt to bed. If he wanted to stay up, he could. Never mind the ache in her chest, because the damned thing was confused. She'd chalk up the pain to heartburn, even though she had no clue what that was, but Grandpa complained about the ailment.

Who knew why Charlot wanted her along? The man was impossible to read. So screw wondering about him. He was a man determined to walk alone. She was apparently an inconvenience to him.

"*Ma chérie...*" His tone caressed her ears.

She squeezed her eyes shut. Like hell she'd allow his sugary voice to pierce through the wall she was attempting to build around her heart. "Yes?"

"You did well today. Very well." A glow came from the *spill* he was using to light his pipe.

She hadn't seen him use that before. He'd probably stolen it from Pierre, along with the additional tobacco. "Thank you."

"I mean it." His voice grew serious. Under the shadows of the fire, he was a mystery, a true enigma she couldn't figure out.

"I know you do."

"I must admit you have proven me wrong many times," he continued his quiet musing. "You are made for this land."

"Maybe I was born like this?" she muttered, picking at the edge of her sleeping bag.

"In what way?"

"To kill." She shrugged.

"No, you do not kill. You defend and protect, just as a true warrior does." His voice warmed with admiration, a true coziness like the welcoming fire lighting the night.

His compliment became a soothing blanket of serenity. But she scolded herself for daring to let his words once again open her heart.

"You are much different from your sister." Admiration soaked his words.

"Do you still find her...pretty?"

"Fire Woman?" Confusion peppered his question.

"Yes."

"Ah...she is a beautiful woman. What man would disagree? But..." He spoke as if he had his pipe in his mouth.

Shivering, Alma forced herself to ask what dared to sit on the tip of her tongue. "But what?"

They sat in silence for the longest time. Only the crackling of the fire and the odd hoot from an owl offered music to the night's stillness.

"She is not you." His answer was softer and quieter than the puffs of smoke drifting from his pipe.

"Explain."

He snorted, something she'd never heard from him before.

"What?" Annoyance crawled along her spine. She almost sat up in the sleeping bag but chose to remain facing away from him.

"You are always so full of questions. A simple answer is never enough for you." He sighed.

If she turned around, he'd probably be shaking his head or rubbing his brow. She adjusted her position to face him. He wasn't doing either but simply smoking his pipe and staring at the fire.

"Well?" She wasn't going to let him get off easily.

"Arms Oneself, does not saying *she is not like you* tell you something?"

"No, it does not. I am aware she is nothing like me. I spent my life being compared to her, and coming up…" She couldn't say *the short straw* because the words wouldn't translate correctly. "Empty."

"Empty?"

"Yes, empty." The frustration in her chest spewed from her mouth. "Everyone loves Fire Woman. As for me, I am the ugly little sister who spends too much time hunting and fishing and not enough time being pretty."

More silence greeted her annoyed ears, and she gritted her teeth.

"I do not believe people expected your sister to sit and be pretty," he began slowly. "Nor do I believe they expected you to try to be like your sister. If they compared you to her, then they owe you an apology. As for hunting and fishing, you are skilled in this area, whereas your sister is not. Does this make her less of a person? No. You are both yourselves with your own special gifts. Nothing more."

He puffed again on his pipe, staring at her. "If I did not find you attractive, we would not have joined as one. What does this tell you?"

Her chest ached. "That you find me…attractive."

"There is nothing else to say," he murmured.

"But if Fire Woman was here—"

"No." His voice filled with annoyance. "You cannot think that way. The fact is, she is not here."

"But if she was…"

"*Mon Dieu*." He shook his head. "What more do I have to say?" His shoulders moved up and down. "I would have had to save her again. Whereas you have more than proven you do not require saving." He tapped his pipe against the rocks circling the fire. "Make me some room."

She stiffened. "What do you mean?"

"You know what I mean. If you are going to keep talking, I might as well bank the fire and rest. It will be a long day tomorrow. Your dog will alert us to anything out there."

She lowered the zipper of the sleeping bag. "We will not both fit. Get your blanket."

He grabbed the two blankets from the makeshift sled. Thedore watched, thumping his tail. When Charlot began to spread the blankets across their sleeping mat, heat gathered between Alma's legs.

He slid under the covers, still fully dressed. As he pressed his body to her back, his rugged, masculine scent enveloped her. Surprisingly, she found the musky aroma pleasant rather than off-putting.

"Sleep," he whispered, setting his palm on her shoulder.

Sleep? With his body pressed against hers and his enticing aroma daring her to face him so their lips could collide? Not likely.

His hand glided from her shoulder and cupped her waist.

She stiffened.

"Easy, *ma chérie*, I mean sleep. I am tired, as are you. We must rise with the dawn and begin our journey once more."

His palm slid from her waist and glided along her stomach, which elicited butterflies, and finally rested on her breast.

Alma sucked in a helping breath. His gentle cupping of her boob wasn't sexual but comforting, even tender. Her lids closed on their own, as if obeying Charlot's gentle order to get some rest.

His lips brushed the nape of her neck.

Not since they'd had sex had he shown this kind of tenderness.

They lay together like two spoons in the drawer, every part in sync—his knees bent with hers, his groin plush against her buttocks, and his chest molded perfectly along her back.

A single thought whirled through her mind, the same one that hovered like a fog refusing to dissipate—maybe she was meant to be here, a woman created to be a warrior within the interior of Canada.

Theodore was doing well. Not starving. Not wishing for the blankets she'd made up for his bed beside hers back home because he was too big for anything else. The wilderness would supply medicine to treat him if he became ill. Dogs had survived out here since time began. They'd thrived on their own until man had thought to domesticate them.

Then there was her family.

Could she stay?

Was she falling in love?

She couldn't fall in love with him. To love Charlot was dangerous. It meant if she returned home, she'd become broken-hearted, mourning a man left back in history, no longer alive.

But if she stayed...

Edie had wanted to stay. She'd been mature enough to make the decision that best suited her.

Alma couldn't live with her parents forever.

She was eighteen, amid her freshman year of post-secondary schooling.

If the education institute hadn't been so close, she would've moved away as Edie and her brothers had done.

"Why do you think so much?" Charlot whispered.

Alma stifled her gasp. "How did you know I was thinking?"

"You are always thinking, and you are very stiff. Get some sleep. Tomorrow is a long day." He moved in closer, resting his face against her short hair.

He was right. Thinking would do nothing but cost her sleep. She needed rest to make the trip to the river.

Chapter Twenty: He Carves His Stone

ALMA GLANCED AT CHARLOT, who stood on a big smooth rock, gazing out at the river.

They'd traveled for three days and had finally reached her homeland, a big river with a snakelike shape moving westward from Rainy Lake to Lake of the Woods, as she knew it in the twenty-first century.

What had captured Charlot's attention stood across the waterway, two men on the opposite shoreline—the United States in Alma's timeline—working a fishing net. By his intense stare, she thought he might know them.

Thedore whimpered.

"Yes. I will take care of it." She wasn't sure if Charlot wanted to remain here or not, but Theodore's whining meant he wished to be unhooked from his sled so he could get a drink and probably swim to cool off.

Once she unhooked him, she approached Charlot. "Do you know those men?"

"*Oui*. I stayed at their village." He never looked at her but continued to stare out at the river, which created the beautiful sound of water moving against the rocks.

Here, the river appeared calmer than in other areas, but she wasn't fooled, aware of the current beneath.

Thedore waded into the water.

"Stay," she ordered him, so he wouldn't swim out too far.

Alma didn't recognize any landmarks, but she had only grown up on this river in the twenty-first century. For all she knew, they could be close to where Hungry Hall one and two had once been located. It couldn't be Long Sault because that was where the rapids were, according to Great-Grandpa. There wasn't any sign of Watrous Island either. They were nowhere near Little Forks. They had to be somewhere between her reserve and the mouth of Lake of the Woods.

Wait, they had followed a small river to reach Rainy River. What if it had been the Pinewood River of the twenty-first century? That made sense considering where they'd come from. They were probably about twenty clicks from the town of Rainy River. The waterway then emptied into Lake of the Woods. She should've known Charlot would have led them along this route.

"We will barter with them," Charlot announced, pointing across the river.

"Barter for what?"

"For mobility. As you can see, we need a canoe. Walking through this dense woodland takes too long. To travel swiftly, we need to be on the water and only portaging when we must." He stuck his pipe into his mouth. "*Ma chérie*, please ready me some fire."

While she used the flint and steel to light the tinder, Charlot rested on his haunches beside her, still staring out at the men who hauled in their catch.

He lit his pipe, grinning at her beneath his lashes.

"What?" She closed the tinder box.

"You are truly made for this land, *ma chérie*."

Because she'd helped him light his pipe?

"You do not require the assistance your sister did." He kept grinning.

Alma's chest warmed. "No, I do not. Grandpa—"

"I am aware all that he taught you." Charlot stood. He waved toward the other shore.

The men returned the wave as they spread their catch on the shoreline rocks.

"They will be over once they are finished up. You will cook them a meal, for they will offer us what they have caught. While we are talking to them, we will barter for a canoe," Charlot announced. "Be sure to hide your footwear and weapon. As for your pants...we will say they were a gift from another trader."

Alma nodded, deciding to follow his lead. Funny, when they'd first met, she'd argued with him about everything, had even questioned him constantly. Now, she had no desire because she needed him to guide them. Was her ego pricked because of this? No.

Maybe Mom and Dad were wrong. She wasn't headstrong and immature. She could listen...when she decided it was the appropriate course of action.

CHARLOT FINISHED THE last of his fish, savoring the tenderness of the sturgeon that the *Saulteur* men had offered and Arms Oneself had prepared.

He glanced to where she cleaned up, not huffing or muttering about having to store everything away, which she considered women's work, probably because she was learning the chore wasn't a duty of a woman but one of survival.

The two men listened, nodding as Charlot regaled them with their plight, a story he'd conjured off the top of his head.

He even informed them that he'd taken Arms Oneself as his new wife over the summer after her village had been attacked by the Sioux. He made the announcement in case one of the men wanted her to be part of the bartering. *Marriage à la façon du pays*—or according to the custom of the country—was practiced here many times over. Charlot had first experienced it when journeying to the interior with his father.

"The Sioux grow bolder," Fishes Many Sturgeons said.

"That they do. I am thankful I was able to spare my wife and I from what happened," Charlot continued. "As for her parents, I do not know what befell them, for I dared not return. I fear the Sioux occupy the village now. To return means death."

"Walks with a Limp and Woman of the Sky were good people," Broad Nose added.

Charlot nodded since the man had referred to Fire Woman's adoptive parents. He'd told them they'd adopted Arms Oneself.

"I could be mistaken, but I heard her name was Fire Woman," Fishes Many Sturgeons murmured.

The blood drained from Charlot's veins. "Ah, a miscommunication perhaps."

Broad Nose wrinkled his brow. "Yes, perhaps a mistake." He glanced to where Arms Oneself continued to clean. "I heard their daughter was a great beauty..."

This time, heat suffused Charlot's cheeks. "Yes, a true beauty." Clearing his throat, he returned his gaze to Arms Oneself.

The look both men cast him said they did not agree.

"I am most fortunate." Charlot stuck the end of the pipe in his mouth. "Most fortunate."

"I believed you would marry sooner or later." Broad Nose grinned, aptly named because of his long, bold nose. "A man cannot stay out here too long without a woman."

Charlot kept watching Arms Oneself. His whole life, he'd held no intention of ever marrying, no matter how beautiful a woman was. Yet, Arms Oneself had crawled beneath his skin and had produced an itch no amount of medicine could heal. She was everything he had not wanted in a woman—stubborn, quick to anger, highly independent, and challenging everything he said or did.

Then why did he find her refreshing? Their journey here had been a quiet one, only talking when necessary, and too exhausted at night to engage in a battle of wills. She'd gone into survival mode, the same as he had, both determined to reach the river as quickly as they could, which had meant trekking through the wilderness, a long, tiring process since they'd been without a canoe.

"As you can see, we have lost everything but what we carry." Charlot motioned at the sled. "I took an injury and needed to heal, which is why we traveled slowly."

"Come with us. We will shelter you for the night." Broad Nose looked to his friend, who nodded. "You can regale the people with your tale."

Charlot hid the big breath he wished to expel. They could replenish their supplies and start anew with what they'd need to survive.

ALMA BREATHED A SIGH of relief, glad she had a moment to organize herself before catching a true view of how her people once lived. She stayed behind while Charlot, Broad Nose, and Fishes Many Sturgeons strode ahead, calling out to the people. This gave her time to hide her boots and rifle with her backpack, buried under the blankets covering the travois Theodore pulled. She also slipped on the moccasins the two men had given to her, both slightly baffled she'd been traveling with only bare feet. They had frowned, though, because her feet remained clean and unscratched.

As she wandered through the camp, she took in people drying berries over campfires on racks fashioned from sticks and twigs. Women were bent over more campfires, cooking. Others pounded dried leaves and plants on flat rocks, making some sort of creamy connotation they'd use later, or maybe something to add to their dinners. Little children ran naked, a few swimming in the water while others dashed about on the rocks of the shoreline.

Many wigwams filled the area, with people flowing in and out of them, some carrying tools, while others were empty-handed. Their clothing, true to what Edie had described, made from animal skins and furs, sucked the breath from Alma. Not so much fur during the heat of summer, though. She also spotted a few blankets strewn over lines tied to trees for airing.

Thedore stayed by her side, even though other dogs ran loose, a few playing with the children while others sniffed out any morsels of food that might be on the ground within the lush grass or between the rocks.

Was Song Sparrow somewhere amongst the crowd? The supposedly stunning maiden who'd befriended Edie. Sadness had flecked Alma's older sister's eyes when she'd described Song Sparrow since Edie had no idea what had become of her best friend after the Dakota attack.

Maybe Song Sparrow had managed to escape and make her way here?

Alma glanced around. There were many pretty young women, but none who possessed the unreal beauty Edie had spoken about. Still, Alma would ask around. Someone must know Song Sparrow.

She gazed up at the blue sky since the area wasn't covered by the canopy of trees.

"Come." Charlot extended his arm.

Alma followed him through the many people. Maidens peeked his way, all of them sneaking seductive smiles, which Charlot returned. A hint of green-eyed jealousy expanded within Alma's chest. No warrior even glanced her way. She shrugged off the disinterest people showed her, even though she wore pants.

Hopefully, Charlot would make the trade quickly, but instinct told Alma they'd have to eat first and possibly spend the night. Her people performed every task at a snail's pace. Not that they were lazy. They simply did not view time in the same way as Western society, even in her time.

Two young girls around sixteen giggled, peering at Charlot.

Alma understood how age worked in the here and now. Even though the girls were young by twenty-first-century standards, in the eighteenth century they were considered marriage material if Charlot chose to speak to their fathers about taking a wife. Pretty squicky, but Alma wouldn't judge. She was living well over two hundred years in her past.

They stopped at a wigwam where a man around Dad's age sat.

While Broad Nose and Fishes Many Sturgeons spoke to the man, Alma stayed behind Charlot but continued to glance about.

"Try to look their way. You know it is rude to ignore them," Charlot whispered, peeking over his shoulder.

Annoyance slithered up Alma's spine, the familiar irritation from him telling her what to do, as when they'd first met. Something she'd assumed she'd conquered, but apparently not. "Understood," she muttered and moved to his side.

A woman Mom's age sat with her knees to the side, hands in a bowl full of berries. She glanced up and smiled.

Alma pushed aside her annoyance and returned the smile.

"You are Fire Woman?" the woman asked.

Alma quickly looked to Charlot.

Charlot placed a hand on her shoulder. "This is Arms Oneself. My wife. Daughter of Walks with a Limp and Woman of the Sky. Wife, this is Tends the Fire."

"You have traveled far. Come inside and eat." The older woman stood, brushing the dirt from her doeskin skirt. "You must be famished."

Alma wasn't since they'd eaten before making the journey to the village, but she could not refuse the food or she'd insult the woman. "Thank you." Even though she wished to vanish, curiosity reared its ugly head since she'd get to see what Edie had witnessed.

Alma followed the older woman into the wigwam. Her eyes almost popped from their sockets at viewing a true ancestral lodge. Before her lay furs for bedding, a cooking fire, backrests made from tree twigs, and rush mats. She was so enthralled, she had to choke back a gasp.

The woman motioned at Alma's pants. "*Ogichidaa-kwe*?"

"Yes."

Delight shone in the woman's dark eyes. "I am honored to have you here. Please, sit. Make yourself comfortable."

While Alma sat, Tends the Fire dished up a stew into a birch bark bowl. She handed the food to Alma.

"*Meegwetch*." Alma dug into the thick stew.

"Forgive me. I was told your name is Fire Woman. But what I heard is wrong. I would be most honored if you feasted with us tonight and stayed before you continue your journey."

What could Alma say? Even though nervousness fluttered in her belly, she would have to continue to play Charlot's fake wife.

Fake.

Then why did she wish it wasn't fake?

Chapter Twenty-one: This is the Time

CHARLOT KEPT A STOIC expression, even though he'd finished bargaining for a canoe. The people were sympathetic upon hearing of the attack by the Sioux, and he'd traded the pipe Arms Oneself had given him for the floating vessel, aware of how the Indians admired such items. But now he'd have to construct a new one, which wouldn't be difficult. He could work on it tonight while they sat around the fire talking.

He and Arms Oneself would be staying the night. He wasn't surprised by Whispers to the Trees' invitation, husband to Tends the Fire. The pair had one older daughter, Blue Jay Woman, residing in their wigwam with her young son after she'd lost her husband a couple of years ago, and they also cared for Tends the Fire's mother.

He entered the wigwam to find everyone seated around the fire, waiting for his arrival, along with Whispers to the Trees.

"Hello, Charlot." Blue Jay Woman sat on the other side of the fire, her smile demure, but the heat reflecting in her eyes said she was more than glad to see him. She held a young boy in her lap, and by his size now, he must've recently left the moss bag and probably toddled about. When he'd last visited, the boy had been learning to crawl.

At twenty summers, Blue Jay Woman was a pretty woman, but her beauty could not compare to Fire Woman's or even Song Sparrow's. He'd previously had his eye on her but had respectfully kept his distance. However, she was a year past the mourning stage after losing her husband to a bear attack.

"You were out picking berries and missed a chance for me to tell you that our French friend has gained a wife," Tends the Fire announced to her daughter as she began ladling up the food. "He brings her with him." Her gaze traveled to Arms Oneself.

Blue Jay Woman nodded, but the smile never reached her big, dark eyes. "Hello. It is an honor to have you at our lodge." Even her words lacked sincere friendliness.

Arms Oneself nodded.

Charlot rubbed his chin. He'd taken Blue Jay Woman for a reserved woman, but she'd been grieving when they'd first met. Maybe she still experienced grief because she wasn't warm and welcoming to Arms Oneself as she'd been whenever he'd visited in the past. However, she didn't seem to have a problem with giving him a kind greeting when he entered the wigwam.

Whispers to the Trees received the first portion of the meal, followed by everyone else receiving a bowl.

Charlot dug into the food, his stomach growling because he hadn't partaken in a meal since early that morning when he'd dined with Fishes Many Sturgeons and Broad Nose. He should have joined Arms Oneself and Tends the Fire when they'd previously eaten.

After the meal, the men moved outside to sit around the fire. While Whispers to the Trees regaled them with some fishing tales, Charlot worked on his pipe, having selected the perfect size branch from an ash tree, not too long but not too short, and not too wide or slim. A few of the children played with Arms Oneself's dog, who raced after them, barking.

Above Charlot, the sky streaked with red, indicating the approaching night. Although the smoke from the fire kept the mosquitoes at bay, those smart enough had slathered themselves in bear grease.

The women emerged from the wigwam to join them.

Arms Oneself headed to the water to clean up items that required washing. At least she'd nodded in obedience when Tends the Fire had asked for assistance. But to decline would've been offensive after the family had shown them great hospitality. However, she might also be learning that what she believed to be women's work was a necessity out here, especially when alone on the trap line.

Blue Jay Woman rounded the fire holding her son and sat beside Charlot.

"It is a lovely evening, is it not?" He used the heated wire he'd removed from the fire to hollow the pith of the branch he worked on. This new pipe would suffice, even though he'd rather have the one Arms Oneself had given him.

"That it is." Blue Jay Woman gazed upward, her smile true, by the sparkle in her eyes. She wet her lips, softly asking, "When did you take a wife?"

Her question sent a slight ripple of shock along his spine. To ask something so personal went against everything he knew about the *Saulteurs*. They were always well-mannered.

"This summer." He never looked her way but concentrated on working his branch. "We have known each other since she became the daughter of Walks with a Limp and Woman of the Sky."

"They are good people. I have met them."

"I do not know what became of them after the attack, or if they even survived. We did not dare return for we believe the Sioux are occupying the village." Charlot held the branch, letting the wire do its work. By the time they readied for sleep, he should have a good start on his pipe.

"Take this." Whispers to the Trees stood before Charlot, holding a shorter smoking pipe he must have traded for at one of the forts, instead of the traditional long-stemmed kind the *Saulteurs* used for ceremony and casual smoking.

Charlot didn't protest. To refuse the object was a true insult, but part of him wished to refuse because already the couple had given him and Arms Oneself so much. "Thank you." He took the pipe.

Whispers to the Trees' dark eyes glittered. "I know how much you enjoy your smoke. Smoke, my friend."

"That, I will." Charlot would finish this new pipe for Arms Oneself, since she now liked smoking. After removing the pith of the branch, he started to carve an intricate design and would subsequently add decorative elements to the gift. He'd also have to select a nice hardwood for the bowl. But that could wait. He had more work remaining.

"Very pretty." Blue Jay Woman leaned in closer, her gaze admiring. "Now you will have two."

"A present for my wife." Charlot lightly chuckled. For some strange reason, referring to Arms Oneself in such a manner rolled easily off his tongue and left a feeling of sweetness in him, whereas in the past he would've balked.

Blue Jay Woman frowned.

Arms Oneself appeared out of the growing darkness, clutching the items she'd washed. As she strode their way, her soft expression hardened.

Charlot didn't want Arms Oneself to see the pipe, so he reached for the blanket at Blue Jay Woman's feet and covered his lap, making sure to keep his head lowered.

Arms Oneself stomping feet, much to Charlot's shock, were loud enough to wake her sleeping ancestors even though she wore moccasins. She huffed toward the wigwam, her doeskin dress, a gift from Tends the Fire, swirling around her ankles. Just as quickly as she appeared, she vanished.

Part of Charlot wished to investigate what had her upset, but he stayed put. To speak intimately in front of guests was considered bad manners. He was sure he'd find a better moment to ask her.

For the rest of the evening, Charlot listened to stories while also talking to Blue Jay Woman, who continued to sit beside him, but Arms Oneself never ventured back outside.

He frowned. They would speak. To ignore story time was an insult to the storyteller.

When Whisper to the Trees finished his last tale, everyone rose.

As they filed into the wigwam, Arms Oneself brushed past them, excusing herself.

Tends the Fire made up a bed of fresh robes. Instead of retiring to his pallet, Charlot crept outside, doing his best not to trounce. At least Arms Oneself had left the wigwam, or they might've embarrassed themselves in front of good company who'd been generous enough to share their home for the night.

He found her standing behind some bushes a good distance away. "What has upset you? You behaved rudely tonight to people welcoming enough to share their food and lodge with us." His building anger came out in his words.

"I was busy working," Arms Oneself fired right back, hands on her hips. "Since you like to speak about hospitality, I was showing my gratefulness by cleaning."

"Cleaning?" Did she expect him to believe such a foolish answer? "It was more than apparent you thought to hide and sulk."

"Sulk?" Arms Oneself sputtered. "What does it matter if I did not join everyone outside? You had *plenty* of company."

"You are supposed to be my wife tonight. Do not embarrass me by behaving like a child." He thrust his finger toward the wigwam. "Get in there now. Tends the Fire has made up our bed of robes."

"I will go nowhere with you." She sneered, folding her arms while stubbornly jutting out her chin.

Mon Dieu! She'd be the death of him yet. "If you do not sleep on our bed, I will personally return you to the dancing flames and shove you in by your backside as I did to your sister." His face was an inch from hers.

Shock, followed by panic, and then anger passed through her eyes. She placed her palms on his chest, as if to shove him.

But her touch, instead of trigging more anger, ripped the lust out of him that he'd buried. It exploded forward. He gripped her by the waist, pulling her firm body against his.

Arms Oneself gasped and then wriggled.

For once, he'd show her who was the man between them. Enough of her constant need to prove dominance. He slammed his mouth down over hers.

She wriggled a bit more, but when he ceased to press hard on her lips and instead skimmed them with tender caresses, her hands bracing his shoulders became a gentle massage.

The heat from her flesh slathered his skin with goosebumps. She was a fierce cat, much like a lynx in the woods, always ready to strike but quick to purr when gently scratched under the chin.

He delved his tongue between her lips, tasting the intoxicating flavor of her mouth. She was sweeter than the berries they'd eaten that morning. He tangled his fingers into her hair, tilting her head upward to mold their mouths as one. Her breasts melted against his chest, and he drew her tighter against him while exploring the heat within her mouth.

His heart raced, and he trailed his fingers along her skirt, stopping at the hem. Temptation clawed at his insides to take her again, to thrust his hard flesh within her wet depths. He glided his fingers along her silken thigh, taking the skirting with him, exposing her to the warm air.

The suppleness of her skin and the strength in her leg created a powerful want in his loins. He used his fingers to create a path from the back of her thigh to the curve of her buttock that flexed from his touch. Caressing her smooth but firm derriere melted his insides. He was consumed by heat, aching for her. When he nudged her legs apart, much to his delight, her tongue searched deeper in his mouth, and her breaths became heavy sighs and moans.

He broke the kiss.

Her eyelids flickered, disappointment in her gaze.

"No. Turn around."

She obeyed.

He locked his arms around her waist, pressing his lips against the nape of her neck. He'd been surprised when he'd found such a tender spot on such a strong woman. Maybe the only vulnerable spot on her. When he cupped her womanly area, the coarse hair teased his palm. She moaned and arched her back, rubbing her derriere against his groin.

He thrust his hips, grinding his hard flesh against her bare bottom.

"Charlot," she panted.

She needed him...her desires whispered in the calling of his name.

With his fingers, he spread her feminine lips apart, slipping into wet heat. She thrust her hips forward, reaching for him. He rubbed her nub, moving in a tiny circle around the sensitive area. The excitement coming from her thrilled him.

He managed to lower his breeches using his free hand, releasing his erection. Arms Oneself continued to grind against him, her moans taunting him, daring him to penetrate her. He eased into her, almost sighing with relief since his sac had swollen with an unbearable ache only breaching her could relieve.

She squeezed his erection with her tight flesh, sucking the breath from him. Her moans grew louder, and he had to slide his hand over her mouth to keep quiet, or others might hear them. He started with slow thrusts, savoring her wet, silky flesh, while continuing to rub the small, hard nub between her womanly lips.

She bucked harder, smearing her wetness all over the tip of his finger.

He suckled on the nape of her neck, the pleasure building in his loins. She was taking him far from the buzzing of the mosquitoes, far from the village, and far from their latest predicament.

He rutted faster, excitement roaring through his veins.

Just as his release washed through his limbs, she also cried out, joining him in the heady sensations.

Chapter Twenty-two: On the Run

ALMA HELD TIGHT TO the edge of the fur robe. The light snores and heavy breaths indicated everyone in the wigwam slept. Only she remained awake. Once they'd returned to the lodge, Charlot had closed his eyes and had fallen into dreamland without even a goodnight to her.

It must be easy for him to dream sweet dreams because he'd probably been thinking about Blue Jay Woman the entire time they'd been having sex. What else would've created such desperation in a man as calm and easy as Charlot?

He didn't love her. And she didn't want his love. Really. She didn't. And she'd keep telling herself so.

Alma rubbed her brow. The ache in her heart swelled. She didn't belong here. Charlot had more than made himself clear that he was a man who desired to traipse through the interior alone. Plus, she'd kill for a bag of Doritos Cool Ranch. She missed her iPhone. What she wouldn't give for a cheeseburger and fries.

However, as much as she ached for things of her timeline, her muscles had grown stronger with each passing day, and the nagging little bump of her lower stomach had vanished. If she hung around a bit longer, she'd have a gym body women would kill for. Not that she'd been out of shape before making her journey to the past. Being an outdoors lover, she'd been fit her whole life.

The canoe Charlot had bartered for rested on the shoreline. She simply had to pack her belongings, change into her original outfit, and take off with Theodore. Did he miss his bed of blankets since he was forced to sleep outside? Dogs were not allowed within the wigwam this time of year.

His whimper carried through the lodge's birch bark covering.

Alma sat up. She'd go see him. Maybe sneak him some of the leftover meat. Shoving aside the furs, she reached for her skirt. Earlier in the afternoon, she washed her pants and tank top. The garments dried on a line strung between two trees. She'd change and leave.

After slithering her way around the sleeping people, Alma crept outside. Thedore trotted up to her, tongue out.

"Here." She slipped him the meat.

He gobbled up the big chunk in one bite.

She scratched him behind the ears, something he adored. "I know you are loving this adventure, but it's time to go home. He doesn't truly want us. I don't even know why he planned on taking us with him to a new trapline for the winter."

Why...that was the biggest question whirling through her brain.

He seemed attracted to her, but with Blue Jay Woman present—who was more stunning and available and making it clear she longed to be Charlot's second wife—he would likely shift his interest to her. Alma sure hadn't missed their cozy bantering at the fire earlier.

The same jealousy she'd experienced upon seeing them, heads bowed, talking quietly to each other, which indicated nobody should join them, gnawed at her chest. She gritted her teeth, determined not to give in to the rising anger.

Screw him and screw this place.

She'd never conform and be an obedient wife to anyone.

Just as Tends the Fire said, Alma was a female warrior, made to take up arms and do battle.

When the memory of killing the Dakota and Pierre surfaced, she clenched her fists. How could she return home after what she'd done?

She bowed her head.

But there wasn't a chance she was staying here.

She'd make up her damned mind once she reached the dancing flames.

This meant canoeing upriver to the mouth of Lake of the Woods. From there, if she wanted to get home, she'd have to face the Dakota. There wasn't a chance she'd make the same trek through the woods she previously undertook with Charlot.

Maybe there was a way she could paddle into the cove without the Dakota seeing her. From what Edie had said, the enemy was occupying the beach Alma had visited many times in the future. She could also park the canoe elsewhere and take a different route to the dancing flames.

With Theodore on her heels, Alma crept to where she'd hidden her backpack and rifle. She retrieved the items and set them into the canoe. Then she trekked back to retrieve her pants and tank top. She donned the apparel before sneaking off with some food.

Once she finished loading the canoe and helped Theodore get into the vessel, she simply needed to shove off.

She looked over her shoulder at the sleeping village.

A figure emerged from the shadows.

Alama gasped.

"What are you doing?" the man with the braided hair asked.

Alma swallowed. She should have known better. Warriors patrolled the village. "I am…Charlot is aware I am leaving."

The warrior nodded. "Safe travels."

This was it.

The warrior stood waiting for her to leave.

There was no turning back.

Alma cursed under her breath.

Mom was right.

She was too damned impulsive for her own good, always reacting first and thinking about the consequences later.

Mom…

The ache in Alma's heart grew.

She'd see her mother again.

Her father.

Her siblings.

Even her grandparents and great-grandparents.

With a good push, the canoe floated as she scrambled into the stern and took hold of the paddle.

The moon offered plenty of light that reflected off the water. Thank goodness she'd paddled this river many times with Grandpa. She'd make her way safely to the mouth of Lake of the Woods, where there'd be more paddling until she got near the small town of Morson. Then she'd travel west on foot to the dancing flames.

Again, she glanced over her shoulder. The ache in her heart expanded.

Screw it.

She wouldn't have regrets. Charlot only gave a damned about himself.

He'd probably wake up happy that he could pursue Blue Jay Woman without Alma hanging around his neck like a big, heavy sturgeon.

She set her paddle in the water. The current beneath took the vessel away from the shoreline. Soon, she'd be far from Charlot.

Theodore faced her, cocking his head.

"You have done wonderfully out here." Why did she bother to speak in Ojibway, anyway? She was alone and could talk like a girl from the twenty-first century.

Theodore whined.

"We cannot go back. To return means paddling against the current, and I do not have the strength to do so. We must go forward. There is nothing for us here."

But was there anything for her in the twenty-first century besides her family?

AT DAWN, CHARLOT CURSED under his breath, glaring at the spot where the canoe had been turned over. After what they'd shared last night, anger simmered in his chest like a stew on the fire, ready to bubble over. How dare she simply flee for the dancing flames, leaving him stranded in the village, especially after bargaining by using his pipe.

Bah.

Good riddance to a stubborn, headstrong woman.

Some of the people lightly laughed.

A few frowned.

Charlot set his hands on his hips. To save himself further humiliation, he'd have to retrieve his wayward so-called wife, return to the village, and show the people he could control a woman he'd love to drown.

He forced himself not to whip around but calmly turned toward Whispers to the Trees who watched.

"My friend, I must ask another favor," he began, striding to the tall man.

"You wish to borrow my canoe?" Whispers to the Trees grinned.

Charlot's face heated. "If you do not mind. I will return your vessel in pristine condition."

"I know you will. Please." Whispers to the Trees motioned where his canoe lay. "Pack what you need."

"Thank you." Charlot did his best not to stomp to the wigwam to fetch his supplies. As for the belongings he'd left near the bush before first entering the village, he'd leave those since he planned on returning not only with Arms Oneself, but both canoes as well.

Once he had what he needed, Charlot shoved off, quickly scrambling into the canoe. He stuck the paddle into the water and set off. Although Arms Oneself thought herself superior to a man, with his strength, he'd easily overtake her, depending on when she left.

The longer he paddled, the angrier he became. Arms Oneself really thought to disappear into the dancing flames. Simply abandon him without so much as a *goodbye*.

Yes, he was angry. He was not hurt. The pain in his chest came from paddling and nothing more.

All morning, he paddled like a maniac, not stopping for a break, no matter how much his arms hurt. With the current taking him along, he moved at great speed. By the evening, he'd reached the mouth of *Lac des Bois*.

He stopped to light his pipe and contemplate his next move. Before him were two long islands with their serpentine outline, one facing him and the other a contour of the shoreline to his right, as if the mass of rocks had broken off from the mainland to form its own home.

He could remain south of the islands or paddle around and crest the northern shores, where an abundance of spruce trees would hide him. The water might be calmer if he stayed on the south side, however, this meant he might encounter the Sioux if they remained in the area. If he went north, though, it promised a safe journey but plenty of waves.

He would veer north. If Arms Oneself had sat here at this same moment, she'd have chosen the same route. Once he finished his pipe, he dug his paddle into the water and steered the canoe toward the north side of the first island.

He kept his eyes and ears open, squinting and watching, but this could be for naught. One thing he learned about Indians—they could only be seen if they wished to be seen. The devils could hide in the forest like the rocks and plants. Arms Oneself's outfit featured black, brown, and green tones with accents of gold, resulting in an effective camouflage.

Perhaps it was an Indian thing to always dress to match the environment.

Maybe he should have dressed to blend with the environment.

BORN LIKE THIS

He kept paddling until he passed the first island without incident. The second island also offered no problems. Before him was the vast expanse of water and a massive island. Again, he could go south or north. South would take him quicker to the mainland. If he went north, he'd have to go around the island and then paddle the canoe channel to reach the southern waters to get to the mainland.

It was best to be cautious and go north, for this was where the village was located. Any wrong move could put him at risk. Even his exposed position on the water before reaching the massive island could put him at risk. But as he kept paddling, he spied nobody, which was strange. Always, people were moving from one of the many smaller islands to the next.

The longer he steered the vessel, the darker it grew, which was perfect. Under the cover of the night, he could sneak about. Still, the Indians might be alerted by his paddling. They had ears like owls.

He floated down the canoe channel and then veered south toward the narrower channel. This led him to the mouth where the lake opened again. Smaller islands were peppered everywhere. He'd avoid them since the Sioux might be passing the night on one of them. Instead, he headed for the expanse of water to reach the mainland. He was closing in fast.

Instinct told him this was the same route Arms Oneself had taken. She did belong out here in the wilderness.

His stomach clenched.

Then why run for the dancing flames?

Why abandon him in the middle of the night?

Hadn't he promised to care for her when he said he'd settle them in for the winter?

He kept paddling, not stopping even though his arms burned.

The silhouette of the mainland came into view. Charlot stepped up his paddling, stroke after stroke until his canoe crested the sand hiding beneath the water, indicating he'd reached the shore.

Breathing heavy and shaking out his arms, he slipped into the water. He didn't dare stand but remained hunched over. No sounds came from the forest as he pulled the bow of the canoe until his feet sank into the sand of the small beach. He spotted a bush nearby where he could hide his vessel.

He pulled on the birch bark stern, tugging the light boat toward the bush. When he attempted to shove the canoe into the hidden spot, he hit something.

He grinned before he could stop himself.

Ah, just as he'd suspected.

Yes, a smart woman. Cunning. She'd hidden the canoe here. He'd have to maneuver his in beside hers and then cover the vessel with foliage.

He'd found her.

She'd bed down for the night.

Something told him she wouldn't travel to the dancing flames until the morning.

Chapter Twenty-three: Follow Me

THE DEW FROM THE TREES dropped onto Alma's face. She pushed away the droplets, cracking open her eyes. Theodore stood above her, licking his chops. He must've hunted something to eat.

"Come," she whispered. Light filtered through the forest's canopy. Dawn was breaking. "We cannot waste any time." She reached for her rifle and backpack. She'd eat some of the stolen dried meat on the way to the dancing flames.

"You have eaten?"

The dog cocked his head, tongue lolling to the side.

"Good boy." She petted him. "We must make haste."

Haste?

Oh goodness, part of her was becoming sucked into this place and time. And the thought of leaving...

She bowed her head.

But how could she stay when Charlot obviously did not want her here?

She could remain, though, having more than proved her capability of surviving.

Rustling coming from the trees froze her spine solid. She clutched her rifle, ensuring the safety was unlocked. Maybe the Dakota were tracking her? Her own people were savvy warriors, able to hide themselves even when standing right in front of a person.

Run or investigate?

Trying to run through what was termed *the bush* could take forever, since the underbrush was beyond thick. But she'd run. There'd be no more killing...unless absolutely necessary.

"Come. Stay down." She pushed forward, using the tip of the rifle to push aside the thick branches as she waded through the woods.

She had a good half-day walk to reach the spot where she'd first appeared in the dancing flames.

More rustling came from behind her.

Her heart picked up speed as her feet moved across the ground faster than the quickening of her fluttering pulse.

She shoved her way through the underbrush. Twigs from the trees slapped her face. Just as she made another hop forward, warm breath blew against the nape of her neck. *Oh my God, the Dakota are closing in.* The warrior's footsteps were almost on hers. Did she even have time to turn around and fire? Or should she keep running?

Fuck it!

She whipped around, finger on the trigger and...

"What are you doing?" she screamed. "You scared the beejeebers out of me!"

Charlot's eyes widened. "Say again?"

Shit, she'd spoken in English. "Why did you not make yourself known? I could have fired first and asked questions later."

Charlot's eyes narrowed. "Perhaps I did not believe you would stop."

"What are you doing here?" Although she growled, her heart skipped faster than a little girl jumping rope. He'd come for her. He'd really chased her down. Butterflies flittered in her belly, and she yearned to throw her arms around his neck. Kiss him.

He cared.

He really did.

He may not have said he loved her, but actions spoke louder than words.

"Why did you not stay at the village with Blue Jay Woman?"

Charlot blinked and gaped at her as if she'd grown two heads. "Why would I do that?"

Oh boy, she'd messed up terribly. He had no clue what she was talking about.

Her own insecurities were responsible for putting them in this mess. Charlot had never wanted Blue Jay Woman. He'd probably been friendly, simply passing the time with the widow. Maybe he'd even felt sorry for the woman.

"I..." She wet her lips.

He raised his finger, eyes still narrow. "What is going on? Explain yourself, for I have traveled a great distance to track you. You owe me the courtesy of the truth."

Although her pride demanded she snap back, one of the responsibilities of becoming an adult was swallowing the damned humiliation and confessing the truth. "I...I thought you wanted Blue Jay Woman," she muttered, gazing down because she did not have the courage to face him, not when her face flamed with pure humiliation.

"Say again?" He sputtered.

Shit, she had majorly screwed up. "I thought you wanted Blue Jay Woman."

Charlot set down his musket and folded his arms. "You believed after what we did, I wanted another woman."

Ouch. Not a question but a statement. He was making this difficult.

"Did I not say we were to winter together and trap?" He drew in his cheeks. Alma nodded.

"Then what does this all mean up here?" He swirled his finger around his head.

A smidgen of angry heat flooded Alma. "Maybe you should be more specific. You think of me as a warrior, almost a man, but I am still a woman."

His gaze traced from her boots, up her pants to her waist, and finally rested on her breasts. "Yes, it is more than apparent you are a woman."

"A woman wishes to be asked. She wishes to hear promises...any kind of promise."

"A promise?" Confusion gathered in his eyes.

How dense was he? Gosh, she wished she could use English. "Do you think I will simply go with you because you inform me that is what we are doing? A woman needs more than to be simply ordered without being asked."

"Ah... I see my folly." He grinned.

Theodore let out a low growl, baring his teeth.

She agreed with her dog and was about ready to wipe the smug smile from Charlot's face.

"You keep me on watch the way the Sioux do." He chuckled. "I must say you are a true delight."

What was he on about?

"Very well..." He started to remove his hat...

An arrow whirled past them and stuck in a tree.

"Move..." Charlot snatched her hand while also taking up his musket.

"Fuck!" was all she could manage, fright spooking the back of her neck, and disgust because she'd misinterpreted Theodore's warning. He hadn't been growling at Charlot...he'd been growling beyond Charlot's shoulder at the Dakota warrior.

"*Mon Dieu*, keep moving. We do not have him in our sight; therefore, we will be shooting at nothing, something he hopes we will do, for he believes we can only load one ball at a time."

The stupid warrior wanted them to empty their cache of ammunition before killing them.

"Why do you say *one*?" Was this what Edie had experienced while running through the bush, getting slapped in the face with twigs, and having the underbrush tangling around her legs, ready to trip her?

"Only one arrow," he replied through huffs of breath.

"Then we can fight him."

"Fight what we cannot see?" Charlot steered them into the nest of poplar trees.

At least in here, they could gather their bearings since the leaves and branches grew high on top, leaving them with only the underbrush to deal with. Nor could the warrior hide, unless he attempted to crawl through the thick foliage, which they'd see because they'd catch the swaying of the bushes since there wasn't a breeze.

"Do you think he has run back to alert his comrades?" She petted Theodore, who continued to growl under his breath.

"I do not know. Your people are brave. They do not believe they need the assistance of others to fight two people. He also believes you are not a warrior."

"But my pants..." She glanced down at the camouflage.

"It does not matter. He might mistake them for leggings."

"What are we going to do?" She almost clung to his arm. But she wouldn't. The fear had now climbed in her throat, demanding to unleash a scream.

"We must keep moving. Come. Your dog will catch his scent." Charlot kept the musket ready. "You go first. I will follow."

"Go first? You mean to the dancing flames?"

"It is where I sent your sister when trouble arose."

"But once I go in, I cannot come back. Fire Woman more than proved this when the flames disappeared after she reached the other side. I am not leaving you." She touched his arm. "I came to help you. Came to rescue you from death. If I leave, you will be in the same predicament. Unlike my sister, I will not abandon you to save my life."

"Your sister was pushed into the flames by me, for she did not wish to leave either," he reminded her.

"You will not push me. I will not allow it." She dug her fingers into his shirt sleeve.

"Then we must journey on." He motioned at her. This time he faced the west.

"We came from that way."

"Yes, we did. That is where our vessels are."

"Can we stay out here and wait for darkness?" They had to formulate some kind of plan. "They are aware we are in the area. They only attack at sunrise."

"Come, we must find a way to stay out of the sun for it will soon grow very hot."

Alma nodded and followed him.

CHARLOT SCANNED THE area. He glanced down at Theodore, who sat on high alert, but the dog's ears remained flat and his nose calm. The mosquitoes had emerged, and he did his best not to slap at them, having left his bear grease in the canoe.

"You know the risk we are undertaking. You can still return to the flames. I can accompany you." He couldn't resist and brushed his fingers along Arms Oneself's short strands of hair.

She gazed at him, tilting her head upward. "I am not returning. My place is here."

He traced her cheekbone, which was smoother than the fur of a rabbit. "Are you sure?"

"You did not wish for me to return, did you? Is this not why you followed me?" There wasn't a hint of smugness or triumph in her eyes.

"Yes, tis why." He rested his palm on her cheek. "But I do not wish to put you in danger, nor could I bear if I failed you."

"Failed me?" Her eyes glittered with questions.

"Yes, failed you. Failed you greatly and failed myself if anything happens to you." His heart would be torn in two if the Sioux dared to kill Arms Oneself.

"Something could happen to you. It is the risk we take by living out here. My people will eventually conquer this land. It will be ours," she assured him. "And we did not take this land by running away in fright. We stood tall and fought for what we believe is ours."

"Spoken like a true warrior." And she was his *Ogichidaa-kwe*. His strong-spirited woman.

"They will believe we went further within the interior. That is where they look for us. Only a fool would return from whence they came."

She spoke wisely. Now might be the best time to make their escape.

"True," he agreed. "Does this make us fools?"

"No." She shook her head. "It means..." She licked her lips.

A blue jay squawked.

A robin sang.

"Perhaps it means we do not wish to be apart." His tongue ached to say more, but he hadn't spoken so intimately with a woman before. "This is why I asked you to...well, told you to join me in trapping this winter." He should have asked. "Arms Oneself..."

She shivered, still staring at him.

"Will you join me this winter in trapping? Will you remain with me?" He kept his palm on her cheek.

"That all depends..." She licked her lips.

"Depends?"

"What do you feel?" She tapped his chest right where his heart pounded against his ribs.

"I feel..." He took her hands in his. "I felt angry when you left me without a goodbye." Why did he find it difficult to speak what resided inside of him?

"Why were you angry?"

"We had plans...so I assumed. I was wrong to assume, which is why I now ask. I ask because I have no desire to be without you. Your company during our time together...it has been an absolute delight. You have found feelings in me that I did not believe existed. With you, I know I can feel more the longer we are together."

"More?" Her voice cracked.

"Yes. More." The tenderness in her gaze pierced his heart. Such a soft expression. Maybe the first time he'd witnessed this woman gifting him such tenderness.

"I, too, want to feel more." She cupped the back of his hand that remained on her cheek with her palm. "I feel things I never felt before with you."

"Then we shall remain together, my strong-spirited woman. All we must do is get to our canoes and break from here. You know we cannot return from the way we came. The rapids will be too strong to paddle against."

She nodded. "I know. I have canoed the river numerous times with Grandpa, and there are spots you must portage your canoe to get to the...the place where my people dwell...in the future."

"Together...we will fight the Sioux if we must." He let go of her cheek and clasped her hand in a tight grip.

She gripped his in return, her bicep flexing. "We will fight together. Let us depart."

Chapter Twenty-four: All That I Bleed

ALMA'S MOUTH DRIED as they headed toward their canoes. She clutched her rifle, throat clogged with fear, but she squared her shoulders and followed Charlot. Thedore shadowed the back of her boots.

She'd stayed quiet in the bush too many times while hunting with Grandpa. Patience was a virtue, but she wasn't scouting for signs of deer. How completely surreal to fight people who were her allies in the twenty-first century. And this war would continue for a good one hundred and fifty years, according to Edie.

As for Edie, Alma couldn't believe her sister had been crazy enough to let a Dakota loose after her adopted parents had captured the warrior. Alma wouldn't have, because in the eighteenth century, a mighty Dakota would attempt to scalp her, no matter if she'd freed the man from certain torture and death, as Edie had.

Alma glanced behind her. Theodore's ears remained peaked and his nose wiggling, taking in the air's scent.

"Good boy," she whispered.

Hopefully, they could make it to their canoes without encountering anyone. She hadn't trekked that far from the shoreline, so covering the distance shouldn't take too long.

Although they hadn't walked far, an eternity seemed to pass, especially with the birds singing, a couple of red squirrels giving their alarm calls, and what sounded like a rabbit rustling in the underbrush. From Grandpa, she'd learned to differentiate what was real and fake, but the Dakota were masters at camouflage, so they could be responsible for the noise, maybe signaling one another.

The sound of water became music to her ears, and she let out the breath she'd held.

"Quick. We must uncover them." Charlot used his chin to motion at the bush where they'd hidden their canoes. "My supplies are also there."

Alma nodded since she carried hers in her backpack.

This was it.

She left the cover of the bush, crawling on her belly to the canoe. Theodore kept to the bush and followed. Thank goodness Grandpa had trained him well. Then again, Grandpa had trained all his hunting dogs well.

She moved like a snake slithering along the thick grass and over rocks. Finally, she reached her destination and used the tip of the rifle to push aside the branches covering the canoe.

Charlot was beside her, also using the end of his musket to reveal his birch bark craft.

Alma had no choice but to stand to continue uncovering the vessel. She eased off her knees, cringing and glancing around. Theodore remained alert, ready to sound the alarm if anything out of the ordinary bothered him.

She removed the last of the camouflage, revealing the canoe. They had to cross over an expanse of water to reach the big island where the channel waited for their escape.

Charlot stood ready by his canoe. "Come," he motioned at her as he shoved the vessel toward the shoreline.

Thank goodness birch bark was light. Alma easily moved her canoe beside his.

"No matter what happens, you keep paddling," he told her in a firm voice. "I will bring up the rear. You will go first."

Alma's beating heart jumped. That meant he'd sacrifice himself for her if anything happened. "You will live. I am not staying here without you."

"We both shall live, but we must make haste. I need you to head north. We cannot go from whence we came, as I told you."

Thedore trotted from the bush and jumped into the canoe.

Alam turned to Charlot. "Take this." She held out her rifle. "If you are going to cover my back, then you need to be able to fire more than once."

Charlot nodded. He handed over his musket.

Forcing herself to move, Alma turned and set the musket in the canoe. If this was the last time she saw Charlot, she'd cry, but she wouldn't allow herself to think those kinds of thoughts. She gave her canoe a good shove and quickly climbed inside, taking up the paddle. Her backpack sat in the middle while Theodore stood at the bow.

"Lie down," she ordered him.

Theodore obeyed like a good dog.

She slipped the paddle into the water and headed north toward tons of islands they could hide behind. Plus, the Dakota were to the south, so they'd be paddling away from the Ojibway village the enemy had invaded when Edie lived here.

Something told Alma she was in for a shitload of portaging. Not fun. But she'd portaged many times in the past, and she could do so again. Plus, she had only her backpack and the musket to add weight, not a load of supplies.

Charlot had also traveled light since he'd only come to retrieve her.

She couldn't help watching the shoreline as she paddled. They'd be going around Brûlé Island, a place with deep water. Then they'd pass Little Raspberry Island and Raspberry Island. At least the Dakota wouldn't be up picking the delicious berries yet because it was too early in the morning. Unless some had camped on one of the two islands overnight to begin their foraging at dawn.

It'd be the women there to forage, but warriors could be present, guarding them.

When Alma made it past Brûlé Island without incident, she breathed a sigh. Two more big islands to go and then they'd be hidden in the maze of smaller islands.

She paddled on toward Little Raspberry Island but didn't spy anyone along the rocky shoreline. Maybe if the Dakota women did occupy the island, they'd bunked down somewhere within the mass of spruce trees.

Finally, she passed the island and continued her way to Raspberry Island. As she paddled northeast, the sun rose above the tree line, reflecting off the water and making it difficult to see. If only she had her sunglasses, but those were back home in the twenty-first century.

The sun's rays caught something shiny for a split second on the island. Alma squinted.

"Get down," Charlot shouted.

Before Alma could duck, a razor-sharp object embedded itself into her side. She cried out, the pain a fire scorching the left side of her waist. Theodore growled, but he didn't rise, no matter if she reached for him, pleading for his help. The paddle slid from her palm. She fought to keep hold of it. If she lost what was most precious out on the lake, for sure she'd die, though black dots had already begun to appear in her vision.

Shots rang out.

Her gun.

That was her rifle being fired. She'd recognize the sound anywhere.

CHARLOT RESTED THE barrel of the rifle against his shoulder. Red filled the water where the two Sioux warriors had fallen. The six women continued to scream, each holding various objects to do battle. But they could not reach him, for they were on the rocks of the shoreline. They'd need to retrieve their canoes to catch him, but he would not allow them that luxury.

They no doubt desired his scalp more than anything.

One even grieved, using a knife to cut off her braids.

Perhaps he'd killed her husband or brother.

He did not have time to panic, even though Arms Oneself lay in the bottom of her canoe, blood seeping from her wound.

Safety was the first thing he must accomplish.

He worked quickly, floating up to the second canoe. The gunwales bumped together. The dog remained on the floor of the canoe, growling under his breath and stiller than a pond on a windless day.

"Marvelous. She trained you well," he whispered. "We must move fast, for your mistress will bleed out if we do not. First, I must tie the canoes together. We will leave this place and hide within the many islands until I can tend her wound to stop the bleeding. Then we must make haste to the first portage."

He had no idea why he talked to the dog, telling it of his plans, but speaking quietly stopped his furiously beating heart from bursting out of his chest.

While the dog watched, Charlot tied the canoes together. He grabbed the rifle from his canoe and set it on the bottom of Arms Oneself's vessel.

More shouts came from the island, but he never turned to look at the women. He pressed hard on Arms Oneself's wound to stop the bleeding, taking in her closed eyes and steady breathing. That was a good sign. She wasn't dying. Only wounded. But if he didn't find a moment to truly tend to her, she would die. For now, he had stopped the bleeding.

Just as he stuck his paddle into the water, a clear voice cried out for him.

"Charlot!"

The voice sounded familiar.

He craned his neck to see a woman being dragged from the shore by the other women. One beating the poor girl.

Again, she screamed as the women tugged at her. "Charlot!"

Mon Dieu! It was Song Sparrow, close friend to Fire Woman, and a lady he'd had his eye on previously, a beautiful woman with the voice of the bird she was named after.

He could not rescue the pretty maiden. To turn back meant having to kill six women who'd no doubt lead him on a merry chase around the island while he hunted them down. And could he hunt them down? Never before had he killed a woman.

Non, he must think clearly, and saving Arms Oneself was his top priority. At least Song Sparrow was alive, taken captive. If they wanted to kill her or torture her, the Sioux would have done so by now.

He kept paddling, murmuring, "Forgive me, Song Sparrow. But if I risk rescuing you, I could lose Arms Oneself. I can only save one for now, but rest assured, I will do my best to come for you. However, I will need many warriors with me, and a healed woman."

Moreso, he had to paddle past two more islands abundant in berries. The Sioux might be taking advantage of the season with more warriors safeguarding other women now that they had reclaimed the area for themselves.

He didn't know how to order the dog to watch the islands, so he simply pointed at the bow. When the dog perched at the front, sniffing and ears alert, Charlot let out a big breath. He might as well use the name Arms Oneself had chosen for the big beast.

He glanced toward the islands as he continued to paddle, but didn't spy anyone on the rocky shorelines. Still, the Sioux could be hiding among the big boughs of the spruce trees or hidden within the vast underbrush.

Water lapped at the gunwales of both canoes. At least he didn't have to deal with big waves here.

The sun sparkling off the water didn't match his grim mood and concern for Arms Oneself. He would have to go through what she called her *backpack* once he got them to safety,

The Sioux would be out for vengeance once they learned of the two warriors' deaths. By now, the six women might be paddling back to the main camp to alert their people. He could soon have many warriors looking for him.

The Sioux might also know where he planned to head, so he could not take the back route to the fort at *Lac à la Pluie*. Also, Arms Oneself would not be able to help portage the canoes. But he knew of a lake where he could hide them. He would paddle them down a river, then follow a narrow stream that emptied into a lake full of pine trees. It was an out-of-the-way spot, perfect to allow Arms Oneself time to recover.

He continued on until he reached the two islands, also abundant in berries. The area was thick with bushes, which almost appeared blue under the sun's morning rays.

"Theodore, watch," he ordered the dog.

Theodore remained perched at the bow, sniffing and taking in the scents.

Charlot stiffened, knowing the Sioux might occupy these islands because of the many blueberries. He could only pray they were not nearby.

Chapter Twenty-five: Forever After

CHARLOT SHOOK HIS ACHING arms and sighed with relief as the canoe flowed from the stream into a body of water. A lake full of pine. A quiet place out of the way where the Sioux might not look. He'd paddled hard all day, and now he could finally find some place to beach the vessels and attend to Arms Oneself.

He kept paddling through the pine trees, keeping an eye out for trouble, until he spotted the perfect place with a small beach. Beaches were rare in this area, and he sent up a silent prayer. Here, they could even build a fire because the lake was enclosed in the forest, far from the main route.

Theodore jumped out first, swimming to the sand.

Charlot also jumped out, hauling the canoes up on the beach. Once he had the vessels settled, he untied the other canoe. Then he emptied out their supplies and set up a hasty camp. All he had left to do was tend to Arms Oneself, who hadn't stirred.

Fear tiptoed along the back of his neck. He'd checked her breathing during his trip here, and although shallow, she was taking in air.

He slipped an arm beneath the bend in her knees and his other arm under her neck. With the gentlest care, he lifted her from the canoe. She moaned, wrinkling her brows, clearly in deep pain as she slept.

He winced, pity rising from his chest. This shouldn't have happened, but it did. Now he had to care for her as she'd cared for him during his injury.

Once he had a fire going to keep them warm, he dug inside the backpack and retrieved the supplies she'd used when he'd taken an arrow. His fingers weren't as nimble as hers, but he managed to carefully remove the arrow and put pressure on the wound. Then he cleaned the area as she had, which meant applying the stinging liquid she'd previously used. Finally, he stitched the wound closed, surprised she had remained silent and slept throughout the process.

He retrieved some water and wet her forehead with the cool liquid, ensuring to spread some around her mouth. When she licked at the droplets, he let out the breath he held, relief filling him. She'd recover.

Theodore sat beside them, tail thumping.

"Yes, old boy, I will see about food."

She didn't have any provisions, and neither did he, which had been poor planning by the two of them. They should have anticipated problems arising since they'd been traveling in the area taken over by the Sioux after the attack on Fire Woman's village.

While Arms Oneself slept, he sharpened a branch to catch fish. With Theodore following, Charlot eased into the water. The dog wasn't going anywhere to hunt, which meant he'd have to supply the meal for them both. Perhaps Theodore was concerned about his mistress.

Once he caught several fish, he hauled his catch back up to where Arms Oneself slept. Hmm, she should've woken by now. He set the fish aside and crouched beside her, resting his palm over her forehead.

Heat almost scorched his hand. She was gaining a fever. This was not good. He wasn't a healer. The most he could do was keep her warm and covered. He dug around inside her backpack and unrolled the strange thing she'd called a sleeping bag.

Once he had her tucked inside, he started a fire. Then he concentrated on building a lean-to for shelter in case rain came.

They could be here for a few sunrises, and would need to stay warm and dry.

He filleted the fish, settling in to cook them on a stick over the fire while Theodore waited, seated beside Charlot.

"I know you are worried, but remember she is a strong-spirited woman. She will survive." He petted the dog's head. Running his fingers through the dog's soft fur soothed the tension in Charlot's shoulders.

"You love her very much." He gazed into her dog's dark eyes.

Theodore stared back.

Charlot sighed. "I know what she asked of me. What she needs from me." Of all the things to talk to—a dog. He kept scratching Theodore's head, staring out at the lake. "When she took the arrow earlier...my heart stopped beating. It truly did." He swallowed. "My pride is too great at times. Thinking I need nobody but myself out here, when your mistress showed me I do need someone."

Fingers suddenly touched his arm.

He almost dropped the stick of fish into the fire. Glancing down, he gaped at Arms Oneself gazing up at him.

"You are awake."

She nodded but winced, clearly in pain.

"Let me get you some water." He set the stick up against one of the many rocks circling the fire.

Theodore barked.

"Hush." He held his fingers to his lips. "Easy, my friend. She is awake, but we must be quiet. Do not disturb her. Let her rest. Come with me to get some fresh water."

He headed for the lake and scooped a tin cup into the water. Theodore also drank. While the dog continued to slurp up some refreshing liquid, Charlot strode back to Arms Oneself.

He settled on his haunches beside her. "Here. Drink." He held her head up and tilted the cup to her lips.

Arms Oneself greedily slurped the water from the cup.

He couldn't help but adore how she threw aside ladylike manners to quench her thirst. Everything about her went against what he knew of proper etiquette for women. "You took an arrow to the side."

"It hurts." She groaned.

"Then sleep. Did you wake because you are thirsty?"

"No. I woke because I heard you."

The lack of strength in her words pinched him with great wounding. He brushed his palm along her forehead. She wasn't his female warrior right then, but simply a woman in pain, fighting off the fever.

"You said there is something to manage pain. Let me know what it is and I will get it for you."

"A white and blue bottle. Retrieve two. That will help." She licked her lips. "Thank you."

"There is no need to thank me. I had to save you, for you saved me. I cannot let a mere woman show me—"

"You live to tease me." She grinned. "I purposely took the arrow so you would not feel inferior to my skills."

"Oh? Is that so? You pretended to need rescuing?" He also grinned, unable to contain his excitement that she was well, only needing rest and nothing more.

"They have taken our home. Chased out my people." She frowned.

"*Oui.* Perhaps this is why you are here? Maybe you will lead the warriors to battle to reclaim the area."

"Maybe. Fire Woman was meant to be here to meet Thunder Bear." Arms Oneself wrapped her index finger around his.

"Do you believe you were meant to be here to meet me?"

"I thought I was meant to save you, but it is much more."

"We will have to return to where you were wounded. You were not aware of what I saw after you had taken the arrow."

"What did you see?" She squinted.

"I saw Song Sparrow, Fire Woman's dear friend."

Arms Oneself's eyes widened. "She is alive? She did not die?"

Charlot shook his head. "I could not help her. My priority was getting you to safety. However, she is enslaved by them."

"We must..." Arms Oneself started to rise and then dropped back down, pain stretching across her face, lips forming a grimace.

"Easy. Yes, we will need to rescue her. But now is not the time. You must heal. Then we must return to your people. Two of us will not be able to save her. Not even ten warriors. They are a full village. We will require many."

"I know." She sighed. Then her gaze turned thoughtful. "You meant what you said earlier?"

"What did I say earlier?" Ah, this one was always full of questions that made him chuckle.

"About needing someone."

He kissed the tip of her finger. "*Oui.* Now that you are here, I hope you wish to stay."

"Do not be silly. Of course I intend on staying." Her smile was warmer than a cozy blanket. "I will miss my family very much." The corners of her eyes drooped. "But I am meant to be here. I told you already—I was born like this, to be outdoors, to live as you do. My great-grandpa and grandpa taught me everything about surviving out here. They taught me because... Maybe *Gitche Manidoo* told them to."

"I am not sure how or why, but I am thankful you came." He kissed her knuckles. "Now you must rest. And I must finish cooking myself a meal. Your dog awaits. He is also hungry."

ALMA SAT UP WITHOUT wincing as she had for the past three days. Thank goodness for ibuprofen. But they'd have to learn how to make proper medicine once they ran out of the precious pills. At least she could now move without her side throbbing with pain.

Charlot was already up. Berries filled one plate, and he held familiar sticks to roast the fish over the cooking fire.

"Did you pick those berries?" She rubbed her eyes. What a dumb question. She must still be half asleep. Where else would he get berries other than from a nearby bush? This wasn't the twenty-first century, where he could buy them at a grocery store.

Charlot's puzzled expression clearly showed his confusion over the question. "*Oui*."

"Sorry." She yawned. "My mind is sometimes still in the twenty-first century."

"Ah. The future." He smirked.

"Please do not start," she warned him, grinning. "Let us forget about where I come from and think about now."

"I most heartily agree with you." He handed over a stick.

"But sooner or later you will believe me."

"I believe you are not from here. As for this future and the dancing flames...I am still not sure what to believe. I know what you possess are things nobody has seen before. If this weapon were available now, I would have seen it." He motioned at her rifle.

He sighed, staring at her. "Maybe what resides here"—he pointed at his heart—"does not wish to believe you do not belong here. Maybe a part of me worries you will disappear as your sister did."

"I am not disappearing." Alma set aside the stick and grabbed his hand. "I want to remain here...with you."

"As I want you to remain here." He brushed at her hair. "You have shown a man who believed he was to walk his life alone, just how much he does need someone by his side."

Her heart leapt. "You do?"

"*Oui.*" His smile was sweeter than the berries. "I may not speak in flowery or poetic words to you, for that is not my way, but I will admit you do make me feel things I have never felt before. When you left…" He lowered his gaze. "You wounded me."

"I did not think you wanted me. You never asked me to stay. You never told me how you feel. A woman needs to hear what is going on in here." She tapped the side of his head.

"Did I not show you how I feel?"

Funny, there was a saying about actions speaking louder than words, and Charlot had more than proven how much he cared.

"Yes."

"A priest resides at the fort northwest of here on *Lac des Bois*, what your people call *Pikwedina Sagainan*."

She gasped. "We just came from there. The Sioux are there."

"No. The priest resides at a fort northwest of where the enemy is camped. But that can wait. For now, we have much to do before we can think about readying for winter and creating a place to live so we can trap furs. We must continue our journey to the fort at *Gojijiing*, then journey on to Whispers to the Trees' village. Also, we must tell his people about Song Sparrow, for there could be many women besides her, taken captive."

"I agree. She is Fire Woman's dearest friend. I do hope the warriors at Whispers to the Trees' village will help." Then she scrunched her brows. "You mentioned a priest. Why?"

"For marriage."

Oh geez, never in her wildest dreams did she imagine she'd marry the man who'd haunted her thoughts after Edie had come back through time and described him.

"But you did not ask?" She sputtered.

"*Mon Dieu.* Only you would demand that I ask." He grinned, taking her hand in his. "*Mademoiselle*, will you do me the honor of becoming my wife?"

Alma's hand trembled. This was it. She was staying. Yes, she wanted to become his true partner through life.

"Well?" Charlot cocked his brow.

"Yes, I will become your wife." If only she could throw her arms around him, but she needed to keep her hand on the ground for support since her side was killing her.

"You do know that for us to marry the priest will want you to become Catholic."

"I am well aware of the missionaries who haunt this land." *My grandpa and great-grandpa both had to attend the Indian Residential Schools to be stripped of their culture and language, then baptized as Catholics. But for Charlot, I will do this.* "They will have their first *sauvage* convert." She snickered.

"You do know why they use *sauvage*, do you not?"

"Yes, it was explained to me once."

His smile became tender. "The priest is a Jesuit. Also French. Just as your language translates a female warrior literally as a strong-spirited woman, for the French, the word *sauvage* means wild, pure, untouched."

Her heart brightened.

"I much prefer the *Saulteurs* meaning of a warrior, for you are my strong-spirited woman."

"I will always be your strong-spirited woman."

The intensity in his eyes darkened. "I love you, *ma chérie*. Is that what you were also waiting to hear?"

"Yes." She almost squealed. "And I love you, too, even when your arrogance and smugness drive me crazy."

"Even when your stubbornness and many questions drive me mad." His grin became coy.

"Then we are the perfect couple."

"That we are."

She looked to Theodore. "We are staying, boy. Once I recover, we are leaving this area and seeking a new place to reside for the winter. A place where we can trap furs."

Charlot nodded. "We can easily erect a cabin next spring. That will not be a problem. But trapping is imperative. We will need the furs for more supplies."

"Just as long as Blue Jay Woman understands you are only taking one wife." Alma held up her finger.

"*Mon Dieu!*" Charlot threw back his head and laughed, shaking his head. "One wife is enough for me. I have no desire to take another as your people do."

His stare grew serious then, brows knitting together. He leaned in, brushing his lips against Alama's mouth.

She returned the kiss, not a hint of regret surfacing. Only anticipation. Excitement about her future with the man who'd haunted her thoughts for so long.

Alma had found the place where she was meant to be. Edie had found her destiny with Thunder Bear. And now, Alma had found hers—back in time with Charlot Baudelaire.

As for now, they were joined by her people's law, but soon, she would have a legally documented marriage and be known as Mrs. Charlot Baudelaire.

Be sure to read the first book in the Maizemerized series from eXtasy Books Inc:

BORN FOR THIS
MAGGIE BLACKBIRD
October 29, 2021

Excerpt

EDIE SQUEEZED HER EYES shut, thrust out her hands, and shuffled into the mirage of rippling flames. Nothing scorched her skin. Only warmth surrounded her. Something feather-like seemed to stroke every inch of her flesh.

She kept walking, arms out and palms facing whatever awaited on the other side. The scent of spruce was present, even buttercups, and the fresh taste of water. Her feet trampled grass and leaves. A bird chirped. Maybe a chickadee, by its sad song. The little black-capped critters usually sang this tune in the early morning or evening.

Maybe she'd walked out of the maze.

Very slowly, she peeled open her lids to nature—everywhere. Spruce towered high above her. Underbrush shot up from the earth. Wild flowers were aplenty. Why, she could've been in the northwest of Ontario. The sun shone bright, its rays beating down on her. The heaviness of the doeskin dress was a tad hot on her skin.

"It is as my vision spoke. She will walk through the flames to join me..."

A man's voice whirled into Edie's thoughts. No, not her thoughts. His rich tone lovelier than a song had penetrated her eardrums. Nor had he spoken English, but Ojibway, and not the *Anishinaabemowin* she studied in class. Koko called the language Great-Grandpa had interpreted for the courts the old language. Even stranger, she understood him.

"*Ishkode-kwe*," he whispered.

Edie blinked. He'd called her Fire Woman. "I...I..."

Oh, heaven help her, standing beside the bush of green where buttercups sprung was the very man who'd haunted her dreams since childhood. His bronzed, long, strong fingers grasped the stems of flowers—the very same hands that had always reached across the mist to her.

Hair darker than a moonless sky was braided into two plaits and parted down the middle. His nose was long and sharp. Eyes that matched the hue of his hair were narrow in shape. Cheekbones capable of cutting diamonds sat high on his oblong face. Lips the shade of poppies, yet very slim, were pursed in a questioning pucker. Never had she drunk in such a gorgeous specimen of the male persuasion before. Machismo seemed to emanate from him.

No. Wait. Wrong word. He wasn't some macho guy like the boys at university. Courage, strength, and bravery sprang from his athletic body. His masculinity originated from the confidence in his straight posture, hard abs, and forward stare.

Again, he held out his offering.

"I'm...I'm not supposed to be here..." Just as Edie smoothed her dress, she slapped her hand over her mouth. She'd spoken the old language. They could communicate. The scarecrow hadn't been a joke or a mirage. This was real. Realer than...

She pinched the back of her hand and winced from the sharp prick.

"Yes, you are to be here." He curiously peered at her hand, no doubt thinking she was insane for intentionally hurting herself. "The Thunderbirds willed this, for it stormed during my entire quest."

"Wh-what?" she sputtered. He'd had a vision about her, just as she'd dreamed about him? "That wasn't a scarecrow. It was *Mandaamin*."

About the Author

AN OJIBWAY FROM NORTHWESTERN Ontario, Maggie resides in the country with her husband and their fur babies, two beautiful Alaskan Malamutes. When she's not writing, she can be found pulling weeds in the flower beds, mowing the huge lawn, walking the Mals deep in the bush, teeing up a ball at the golf course, fishing in the boat for walleye, or sitting on the deck at her sister's house, making more wonderful memories with the people she loves most.

Web Site: *https://maggieblackbird.com/*
Facebook: *https://www.facebook.com/maggieblackbirdauthor/*
Bluesky: *https://bsky.app/profile/maggieblackbird.bsky.social*
X: *https://x.com/BlackbirdMaggie/*
Goodreads: *https://www.goodreads.com/maggieblackbird*
BookbBub: *https://www.bookbub.com/profile/maggie-blackbird*
Instagram: *https://www.instagram.com/maggieblackbirdauthor/*
Newsletter Sign-Up: *eepurl.com/gJu2VL*